Cowboy Coming Home

Coming Home to North Dakota Book Two

Jessie Gussman

Acknowledgements

Cover art by Julia Gussman
Editing by Heather Hayden
Narration by Jay Dyess
Author Services by CE Author Assistant

Listen to a FREE professionally performed and produced audio-book version of this title on Youtube. Search for "Say With Jay" to browse all available FREE Dyess/Gussman audiobooks

Contents

Chapter 1

Do not be unequally yoked. Light can't mix with dark. Be God centered. God always first. Communication, commitment, loyalty, listening to each other's viewpoints and settling disagreements before going to bed.
- Ruth Carter Warrenton from VA

Glory Baldwin didn't see the calf.

That was the problem.

Although, to be fair, the calf wasn't there when she put the cow in earlier.

Regardless, she should have been paying attention, but her sister Lavender had shouted, "Three more trailers just pulled in. We need that cow moved right away, and you need to come out and help us."

Glory had waved her hand, letting her sister know she'd heard, then she'd gone about moving the cow.

People were milling around in the penning area, but they were mostly people Glory knew, and they knew to stay out of the way when they were moving animals. The livestock auction that her family ran was scheduled to start ten minutes ago, but typically they didn't start on time. Usually people were still arriving with their animals at the start time.

Which is what was happening now, and Glory needed to move this single cow into a pen with several others so they had this pen for a herd of goats that was on a trailer right now waiting to be unloaded.

The new guy had put the cow in, and he put it in the goat area. Which had been fine before the goats had arrived and needed it.

Glory wasn't watching when she opened the gate and walked in the pen. It was way too big for a single cow anyway. They used it for goat herds.

Making a note that the light bulb above the pen was out, and it would need to be replaced tomorrow, she walked in, glancing out of the pen and down the aisle at her sister who was heading toward the unloading area.

Maybe the dim lighting was the reason she didn't see the calf lying in the straw.

Wet, but with the afterbirth cleaned off.

"Look out!" a deep male voice said, drawing her attention away from the calf that had just caught her eye—her brain hadn't had time to process what it was and where it came from—and toward the voice rather than toward the cow.

Out of her peripheral vision, she saw the cow coming for her.

Sometimes things happened and it felt like they were happening in slow motion in a person's head, while real life never slowed down.

That was one of those times for Glory. Since she knew the cow was coming, and she knew her feet needed to run, but she hadn't gotten the signal from her brain to her feet, and she stood rooted to the floor for what felt like five minutes but was probably only a second or so.

A body came from her left, plowing into the neck of the cow, just as the black head came within inches of Glory's stomach.

Her feet finally got the memo, and she ran to the side of the pen, one foot on the bottom board, but she didn't throw herself over; instead, she glanced over her shoulder to see what became of the person who had attacked the cow that was attacking her.

Later maybe she would shake her head over that one. Working in a sale barn, she would have said she'd seen everything.

This wasn't the first time she'd been attacked by a cow, but it probably was one of the closer times, and all because she hadn't been paying attention.

Growing up, her dad always, always told her, "Keep your eye on the cow. Don't ever take your eye off the cow."

She hadn't listened.

It hadn't gotten her, but some other one might.

The man, tall, wearing a T-shirt and faded jeans, with square-toed cowboy boots, and a ball cap, had run into the cow, knocking her off course enough for Glory to get away.

But the way the cow had turned when he hit her had knocked the man off balance, and Glory turned in time to see him sprawled on the ground, rolling immediately toward the fence.

Smart man, not taking the time to get up. Except, this was the goat pen, the fence was farther away than it usually was, and there wasn't enough room between the boards for the man to get through.

The cow, truly upset and scared now, and driven by instinct to do anything to protect her baby, stopped, glanced at the calf on the ground, then back to the man.

She lowered her head and ran toward him.

Glory saw it, but the cow had smashed the man into the fence as he'd started to stand to get over it and ground her head into his rib cage before Glory got a shout out of her mouth and was able to move herself forward.

She thought she heard a crack, but she hoped she was wrong. Because it was almost certainly the man's ribs.

Knowing that it should have been her getting smashed into the fence, if the man hadn't saved her, she couldn't turn away, even though the mama cow was scared and would almost certainly attack her as well.

At least she was on her feet and had a decent chance of getting away now that she was paying attention.

Hopefully, she could at least get the cow turned around. Surely, the shouting would get someone coming toward them. Someone to help, and if the man couldn't get himself up, someone would be there to drag him away if she could keep the cow away from him.

Her movement caused the cow to look at her but not leave the man. Glory knew what would draw the cow to her. She switched directions, and rather than lunging at the cow, she took three steps toward the calf.

The mama wanted to protect her baby, and nothing would draw a mama like something going toward her precious little one.

That was the instinct driving her now. And that was the instinct Glory played on.

She was no match for a sixteen-hundred-pound cow. But she liked to think her brain was bigger.

She was using it now, because brute strength wasn't going to get her anywhere.

Sure enough, the mama swung around, faster than one would think a clumsy cow would be able to swing, and charged toward the human by her baby.

Glory got out of the way, backpedaling as fast as she could. She smacked into the fence, her hands automatically gripping it and her foot going to the bottom rung.

The cow didn't chase her, standing over her calf, and she stood where she was, trying to see if the man could move.

The cow was in her way.

"Come on, mama," she said. "Come get me." She wasn't taunting. Well, maybe she was. She felt pretty secure in her position—secure that she could get over the fence before the mama got to her. But she didn't really want the mama to do that, because she'd want to turn back toward her calf right away, and the man might catch her eye.

Moving a little along the fence so she could see around the side of the cow, Glory caught movement in the dim back corner. At least the man wasn't dead.

She hadn't really thought he was, since the cow had gone after his chest.

That wouldn't kill him right away.

It would be more of a slow death.

He'd end up in the hospital with pneumonia, a punctured lung, internal injuries, and he'd never get better but just fade away.

Even strong, young, and healthy men sometimes couldn't pull through when their chest was smashed.

She'd seen it.

Thankfully, this cow didn't have horns, or the man might need an undertaker rather than an ambulance.

The cow hadn't moved, and Glory could see the man was up, one arm crossed high over his stomach, like he was keeping the pain in, and standing slightly hunched over, like straightening hurt, and he just couldn't do it. But rather than going to the gate or throwing himself over the fence, he was looking for her.

"Get on the other side," he said, his words strong but laced with pain.

Like a sturdy metal gate that was slightly rusted.

"I can make it before she gets to me," Glory said right away, not wanting the cow to turn around. She stood over top of her calf, and she'd probably be fine as long as no one made a move toward her. "You get out of there."

"You first," the man said, his tone commanding and brooking no argument.

She probably knew him, although she hadn't gotten a good look at him and still couldn't see, but most likely he was a rancher from the area. One she'd dealt with before. One whom she might even have gone to school with, although he definitely wasn't someone she worked with every week.

She'd recognize all of those; they were as familiar to her as her own brother.

Shoving her heel on the first fence board, she pushed up, keeping her face toward the cow, not giving her back.

That was the worst thing a person could do when they were chasing cattle and were worried a cow was going to charge—to give a cow their back. Cows might charge a person facing them, but they definitely would charge a person's back.

Apparently they'd never watched westerns.

As soon as her butt was on the top rung, she called out, "I'm good. You get out."

She wanted to be there if the cow moved or turned, because the man was in no condition to get away.

He glanced up, his face dark under his hat, but she could see the stubble and the dark eyes. He made sure she was out of danger before he climbed the fence, much slower than she had, swinging a leg over. Even from her position on the other side of the pen, she could see the pain he was in as he moved his body.

As soon as he had one leg over the fence, she figured at the very worst he could roll off the top, over to the other side, so she swung her legs around and hopped down, moving through the pen she had just landed in, past a herd of goats, who moved out of her way, hopping over that fence before she came around to look at the man.

The whole time, she was pulling her phone out of her pocket and calling Clint, who didn't miss an auction and was also a volunteer first responder. If a person in Sweet Water called the ambulance, he'd be the one going to get it. It seemed silly to call 911 to have an ambulance dispatched when Clint was here and could take this fellow to the hospital in his truck with the flashing blue light.

"Yeah," Clint answered his phone.

"Come down to the goat pens, please. I've got someone who's been smashed by a charging cow, and I think he probably has some broken ribs and possibly other injuries."

"On my way," Clint said, and she didn't bother to say goodbye, knowing he wouldn't.

"If that was for me, you're wasting your time," the man muttered as he came to the fence of the pen he was in, the two nannies who stood there with him eyeing him balefully.

"You're hurt. You need to get checked out."

"I'm fine," he said.

She wanted to roll her eyes. That was typical of men around here. They were "fine." They might have a severed artery and a knife sticking out of their heart, but they were fine. Always fine.

Like it was a badge of honor to not go to the hospital.

"Well, you're gonna have to get through my mom, because she's not going to want to find out that you got attacked by a cow and didn't go to the emergency room."

"Send her to me. I'll let her know," the man said, raising his eyes and looking for the first time full in Glory's face.

Armstrong Brandt.

She knew him, although he wasn't a regular at the sale. His wife had left him last summer, going back east, because she didn't feel fulfilled being a wife and mom and being stuck at home.

Maybe there was more to the story, but that's all Glory had heard. Immediately she started looking around for his little boys. Four of them. The oldest being six or eight. She wasn't sure.

And there they were. She'd been on her phone, and she hadn't seen them smashed back against the pen on the other side, their backs flush against it, their eyes wide.

Their dad had probably told them to get back and stay there, and the boys had listened.

"If you're worried about your boys, we can keep an eye on them. Someone will take care of them." She stopped short of saying she would do it herself. He might not appreciate that since she was the reason he was hurt to begin with. Also, of all the people in their family, Rose was the one who was great with kids. Not Glory.

They seemed to love Rose naturally, even if they'd never met her before.

Glory, not so much. She wasn't terrible with them, but it wasn't an automatic love as soon as they set eyes on her, the way it always was with Rose.

The man scrunched his face up. He'd gone through the gate of the pen and now stood in the aisle.

It wasn't hard to see from the set of his shoulders and the tension on his face that he was in a lot of pain.

"I take it Armstrong is the one who got attacked?" Clint said as he walked up to them.

"That's right. She got him pretty good. He was twisted, and she shoved him into the fence," Glory said, describing it as best she could, even though she'd seen it over her shoulder.

"I'll be fine. My ribs are a little bruised, but they'll be fine."

"I thought I heard a crack," Glory said.

Armstrong's eyes flew to hers. Like he had known about the crack but hadn't thought anyone else had heard.

"Then we definitely want to check that out, especially if there's a possibility they might be broken. You don't want to pierce a lung or get an infection. You can end up with more problems than just broken ribs," Clint said seriously, although he stayed with his hands in his pockets, a casual stance, because he knew as well as Glory did how stubborn men around the area could be. And that he was just as likely to not have a patient to take to the hospital as he was to have one. Unless they were unconscious, it wasn't a given.

"I'll be fine," the man insisted, a stubborn tilt to his chin, his eyes hard.

She'd heard Armstrong's ranch was successful, and she'd never heard of any problems associated with him, other than his wife walking out.

"What's going on?" Mrs. Baldwin, Glory's mom, stepped up.

"Nothing."

"He got smashed into the fence."

"I think Armstrong needs to go to the ER."

Armstrong, Glory, and Clint all spoke at the same time.

Mrs. Baldwin raised her brows and looked around the little circle.

Her eyes landed on the boys that still stood against the fence, worried looks on their faces, with the oldest holding the youngest close to him in a brotherly embrace.

Her serious gaze returned to the man holding his ribs. "Armstrong, I know you don't want to hear this, but I really want you to go to the ER. It has to do with our insurance. They will check you out, and if there's nothing wrong, they'll send you right home. In the meantime, Glory will make sure your kids are okay. She's good with children, and kids always enjoy the sale anyway."

"My kids will enjoy the sale, but I don't want to leave without them." His teeth gritted. "I wasn't staying around much longer anyway, because they need to go home and get to bed."

"I'll make sure they get home. I'll make sure they get to bed, and I'll stay until you get back," Glory said. With her mother's blessing, she would take care of this and see it through until the end.

"The two oldest have school in the morning."

"I'll make sure they get on the bus," she said reasonably.

"If I call the ER, and they're waiting on you when we get there, it won't take long. An hour, two, tops. It's a small hospital, and they know how the people around here are. They don't mess around for the sake of messing around." Clint's words were the nail in the coffin, because Armstrong lifted his chin and jerked it a little in assent.

No one had a problem recognizing that for acquiescence, and everyone moved.

Armstrong, his arm still around his upper stomach, his face still pinched tight, walked over to his boys.

Glory's mom moved back as Glory followed him over, taking a deep breath and hoping she didn't look scary to the little kids. Wishing Rose were here. At least until they got used to her.

"This is Miss Glory, and she's going to be taking care of you, probably at least until bedtime. I should be back by morning, okay?"

The oldest nodded. The second tallest boy scrunched his face up, but when he saw his older brother nodding, he did too. The younger two just looked scared.

"I promise I'll be back. Okay?"

At the looks on the boys' faces, Glory's chest pinched. She remembered that Armstrong's wife had left, and probably the boys worried that he would leave and not come back, too.

It made her sad and also made her determined to do her very best for these little motherless children.

"When you're with me, you get free food, so if you guys like hamburgers and French fries with cheese or ketchup, I've got you covered," Glory said, not sure if that was the best way to talk to kids, but food always made her feel better.

The boys just looked at her, none of them moving to come with her, as Clint checked Armstrong and her mom stood still, giving them time to adjust a little.

"There's also cake, and I know where they hide the candy," she said in a conspiratorial tone.

That made the oldest one smile, although his hand squeezed tighter around his little brother.

"There's candy?" the second oldest said.

"There sure is. What's your name?" she asked, figuring that she probably ought to find their names out before their dad left, since she might not be able to understand them or figure it out herself.

"Benjamin," the little boy said.

That shouldn't be hard. The second child was named Benjamin, second letter in the alphabet. She was terrible with names, always had been, and felt a little pressure, because she really needed to get this right.

"Nice to meet you, Benjamin," she said, holding her hand out.

Benjamin just looked at it for a minute. A cow mooed from somewhere down the aisle, and behind them, a couple of goats baaed.

"Nice to meet you," he said, shaking her hand.

"That's Adam," Armstrong said. "And then you have Caleb and Daniel. Alphabetical." There wasn't any emotion in his voice at all.

She wondered if it was deliberately devoid because of his wife? Or maybe he was just an unemotional person. Maybe that's why his wife had left.

Regardless, she held her hand out to each individual boy. Adam shook it, but Caleb and Daniel just looked at her.

"Let me guess, you guys are four, six, eight, and ten?" she asked, taking a wild guess.

"No. I'm eight," Adam said seriously.

"And I'm six," Benjamin said.

Caleb held up four fingers, and Adam shook Daniel's shoulder, whispering loud enough for everyone to hear, "Tell the lady how old you are."

Daniel stuck a thumb in his mouth and held up three fingers with the other hand.

They were pretty close in age, but Glory's sisters, along with Coleman, her brother, had all been close in age as well.

It made it harder for the parents, which is something she understood as she got older, but much nicer for the kids who had built-in playmates in their family.

"You think everyone's going to be okay if we hit the road now?" Clint spoke loud enough for everyone to hear.

"Yeah. You guys gonna be good?" Armstrong said, his voice holding that same tender tone that he had when he talked to his kids, so different than when he talked to the adults around him.

They nodded stiffly, the anxiety still on their faces, as Armstrong straightened and ruffled the hair of all of them before looking at Clint.

"Let's go." He started walking toward the door, strides that probably would have normally been straight and strong and confident crimped a little from the obvious pain he was in, and his arm still wrapped around his stomach. He leaned forward slightly as well, but otherwise, it was hard to tell that he'd been hurt.

"I'm concerned he might go into shock," her mother said from beside her.

"I've been thinking the same thing. He seems like he's not in much pain at all, but I'm almost positive I heard a crack, although I suppose it could have been a board. I didn't check. I think he's a lot worse off than he's letting on."

"They always are," her mother said, shaking her head.

Her mom had built the auction and livestock business with Glory's dad. When her dad died, she'd taken over, dealing with everything, with Coleman at her side and the girls helping in everything they did.

They didn't stare as the men walked away but turned toward the kids.

"I need to get back to the paperwork if you have these boys?" her mother asked.

"Yeah. We'll be good. I was trying to move that cow out. When she came in, it was just her, but now it's her and her calf, so it's gonna be a little more complicated to get her moving around."

"Yeah. We might have to hold her for a week. I don't think we're going to be able to run them through the arena, and we probably don't want to anyway. I'll check her number and talk to whoever brought her in." Her mom walked over, looking at the tag on the cow's back and pulling out her phone.

Probably to write the information down.

"Have you boys seen a calf before?" Glory asked, assuming that they probably had, since they lived on the farm with Armstrong, but she couldn't remember whether he'd been a crop farmer, or whether he had had pigs or goats or something else.

She just knew she'd seen him before.

"Not one that was just born," Adam said.

"Well, this one was just born in the last hour. Because the mama came in, and it was just her. Now she has a baby."

"Can she break through the fence?" Benjamin said.

"No. These boards are pretty sturdy. But you don't want to put your arm or hand through the fence. Make sure you stay back. Just look through the cracks."

The mom would probably be okay as long as no one tried to get close to her baby, although sometimes cows would get a little crazy when they were penned up. Especially with a little one to protect.

At the very worst, the kids might get their finger smashed if they were holding onto a board, but as long as they didn't stick their head through, they'd be fine.

The boys lined up along the fence, careful to stay back, Adam still holding on to Daniel.

They stood and stared at the cow. She'd licked her calf. He was trying to stand, but she paused and looked at them, her eyes deceptively placid.

"It can't stand up. There's something wrong with it," Caleb said, and those were the first words he'd spoken. For four years old, she thought he talked pretty well, but she hadn't been around a whole lot of children other than helping Rose with her Sunday school class and occasionally teaching junior church.

"It's brand new. It has to learn how to stand up," Glory said, and then she added, "Do you remember when Daniel was born? He couldn't stand up."

"No. I don't remember that." Caleb looked at his brother like the idea that he once upon a time hadn't been able to stand was outrageous.

Daniel had a thumb in his mouth and leaned back against Adam.

They stood and watched the calf for a little bit until it was able to get up. Standing on wobbly legs, it looked so adorably confused that it had been safe and warm just moments ago, and now the coldhearted world intruded.

The boys seemed to get a little restless though, so she asked, "Are you guys hungry?"

She got some nods, so she said, "Can I carry Daniel?"

"Daniel. Let the lady carry you," Adam said, pushing his little brother.

Daniel pushed back against Adam, and Glory grinned. She probably wasn't going to get him to trust her enough to let her carry him around.

"My name's Glory," she said, figuring they might not have heard their dad the first time and they could at least get that so they didn't have to keep calling her "the lady."

"Can I carry you?" She bent down a little to Daniel, deciding she wouldn't know if he'd let her unless she tried.

To her surprise, Daniel took another look at her, sucked on his thumb, and walked the two feet slowly toward her.

She was able to pick him up, grab a hold of Caleb's hand, and herd the rest of the boys out of the aisles.

Whatever they were going to do with that cow and calf, whatever they were going to do with the herd of goats they needed to move, didn't seem to be her concern anymore.

Maybe, if she had time as soon as she got the boys some food, she'd text Lavender and Orchid, her twin sisters, and let them know where she was. But her mom had probably already taken care of it.

These boys were her project tonight; they were worried about their dad and feeling a little lost. She wanted to help them as much as she could.

Chapter 2

Communication is a must
— Sheila Hutchison

A rmstrong slowed his pickup, parking in front of his house and sitting for just a moment.

The pain in his ribs was about the worst pain he'd ever felt. But he hadn't allowed them to give him any hard drugs because he wanted to be able to drive home.

The doctors had been concerned about shock, he learned after he'd been there for a while, although he hadn't realized that when he first walked in. He thought the ribs were the important thing.

They weren't broken, just cracked, according to the x-ray. Three of them.

His lungs were fine, which he had known they were.

Now he needed to go in and figure out how to get rid of the Baldwin daughter.

He supposed she should stay until morning. He felt bad sending her away at—he looked at the console which hadn't blanked out yet—1:30 in the morning.

He probably should pay her, too, although it wasn't like he'd had a choice about her helping him.

Still, she'd given of her time, and he appreciated it.

At least he'd fed the stock before he left for the auction. That was always a good idea, and tonight it had paid off.

The idea of going out and feeding the stock in the morning made him want to cringe, but when something needed to be done, it needed to be done.

There wasn't anyone else around to do it for him, and he might as well face the fact that he'd be doing it. Pain or no pain.

He grabbed the bag that he'd been given at the ER. It contained some of the pills they wanted to give him then, but he'd talked them into allowing him to take them with him, to take tonight so he could sleep. It went against their protocols, but he'd been stubborn, and they'd given in.

He had prescriptions he needed to fill in the morning, and he figured he'd probably do it, as much as he hated pain meds. He didn't want to become addicted to it, heard too many horror stories about people who had, but he needed to be able to function. To take care of his farm and his kids.

Drat Blanche anyway.

If he had a partner, a wife, he wouldn't be facing such a hard task.

Wouldn't have been facing it for the last year.

He had no idea how he'd survived the rest of last summer after she'd left in July.

At least the first crop of hay had been in.

Using his right arm to open the truck door, because his left side just hurt too much, he got out gingerly, into the cool night air.

It might be May, but in North Dakota, nights were still chilly.

He didn't mind; in fact, he'd take the cold over the heat any day.

Walking to the house, he opened the door, trying to figure out whether he should be as quiet as he could so he didn't wake the girl up, or whether he should make some noise so she didn't pull a gun on him.

She was that type of girl.

Glory.

What kind of name was that?

Maybe it was short for Gloria. He'd heard of people named that.

But if he recalled correctly, all of her sisters had flower names, so maybe it was short for some kind of flower.

Morning Glory.

That was the only one he could think of, and it popped into his head right away, because his mom had planted some eight years ago when he'd bought the farm, down along the edge of the porch.

Volunteers came up every year, and they were a deep purple color with a little yellow inside of them.

Pretty flowers.

A little more delicate than the woman with the name, if that's what it was.

"Were they broken?" Her voice came out of the shadows of the kitchen as he closed the door behind him.

It didn't sound like she'd been sleeping. Her voice was soft and free of any trace of sleepiness and not rusty from disuse.

"Three cracked," he said. "How did the boys do?"

Maybe his words were a little clipped. Blanche had been a woman just like this one, tough yet sweet. Well, maybe sweet was a little too much. She had been beautiful at least. But she hadn't been the kind of woman who stuck things out.

He didn't know whether this one was or not, and he really didn't want to find out.

Getting burned once like he had was enough.

"After you left, Daniel thought about it for about five seconds, and he came right into my arms. Didn't want me to put him down for the rest of the night. Caleb held onto my hand like it was a lifeline, and Adam gave me commentary on what all the boys ate or didn't eat, and when we got here, he told me who slept where, and what jammies they wore, and a lot of other things that I probably didn't need to know."

Armstrong bit back a smile and blew out a breath, looking away.

He could just hear Adam rattling on now. Probably this woman that he barely knew knew his entire life story, at least according to what Adam knew of it. Adam was helpful, had great common sense, and Armstrong looked forward to the day when they could work side by side. But he also talked pretty much nonstop. To anyone who would listen.

"Sorry about that. You probably know a lot more about me than you wanted to."

"No. Not really," she said. Not really saying what he had said, and not easing Armstrong's mind at all.

Regardless, it didn't matter. Adam wouldn't lie, and the truth was the truth.

Like everyone else in the world, he had things he preferred the world not know.

"I don't want you to have to go home so late tonight. That's a forty-minute drive, and I wouldn't want you to fall asleep."

"I'm not sleepy," she said, standing up from the chair she'd been sitting on in the corner by the lampstand and coming out into the dim light of the sink.

Whoever built this farmhouse had built a huge kitchen, big enough for all the kitchen things, and he had a little desk in the corner where he did his accounting work for the farm.

That's where she'd been sitting.

It was a rolltop desk, and the top was closed.

He supposed she might have gone through his stuff, and there wasn't anything he could do about it if she had, but he doubted it.

Small towns were notorious for gossip, but they were also notorious for producing people with character, and this woman seemed to have that.

"How much stock do you have?" she asked, standing with one hand shoved in her pocket, one hand hanging down at her side.

"A hundred head," he answered automatically, wondering why in the world she would care about that.

"Is someone coming out to help you in the morning?"

"No. I got it. I'll be fine. They gave me some drugs, the good stuff. I'll take them before I go out."

"Do you have something to take tonight before you lie down?"

Suddenly he felt tired. He hated to admit that a wave of dizziness washed over him, but that was what it was.

There hadn't been any shock to speak of in the hospital, but now he felt like he was going to collapse. Maybe it was a delayed reaction, or maybe his body was just telling him he'd been strong long enough and he needed to rest.

He sat down at the table, his ribs pinching hard. He hated to do it while she was still standing, everything he'd been brought up to be rebelled against that, but he sat anyway.

"No. I have some for tonight, but I'll have to go and get more in the morning. After I get Adam and Benjamin on the bus."

"Then I'll stay. I'll help you get the kids on the bus, and I'll help you feed. I can even pick up your meds if you need me to."

"No. You've done enough. I appreciate you taking the boys. I don't like to leave them with people I don't know, in fact, I never do." The only time he'd left his kids was when his mom came to watch them. She had used her vacation last year, all four weeks of it, to watch them after Blanche had left. That's why he'd been in town today; summer vacation was coming, and he needed someone to watch them.

He'd asked around, hadn't gotten any answers, and stopped at the auction on his way out of town, figuring the boys would enjoy watching it for a little bit.

He hadn't intended to leave there with three cracked ribs.

"No. My family would kill me if I left you with cracked ribs and four boys to take care of. You asked me if I wanted to stay. I do." She grinned a little, like she was saying, "hey, I'm not imposing, because you offered."

"It was just a polite offer. I didn't expect you to take me up on it." Was he joking? He had never been a goofball, but he'd always had a sense of humor. Up until Blanche walked out. That seemed to have been something she'd taken with her, along with her share of the farm. Actually, more than her share, because she'd made him split every single thing they owned in half.

Everything except the kids. She'd given all of them to him.

She hadn't wanted to be encumbered as she reinvented herself.

"Are you okay?" Glory asked, softer, compassion in her voice, as she took another step forward.

She stopped, several feet away from him, and did not reach out, but bent forward just a little, as though leaning down, ready to help.

"Yeah. I'm fine. Just in pain. Which they tell me is normal. And it's going to be my normal for a while."

"Yeah. Broken ribs are hard. Especially because it's hard to find a comfortable way to lie down to rest. I... I never thanked you for what you did. It would have been me right now with the broken ribs and who knows what else, if you hadn't sacrificed yourself."

"Don't say it like that. It's not like I died."

"You could have. You know you could have. Or I could have."

They both knew it. That was just a fact of life on the farm. There were a lot of dangerous situations, and sometimes people were killed.

"I didn't know that cow had a calf. When we put her in the pen, she didn't. And it was my fault, because I wasn't paying attention. Because of my lack of attention, you had to go to the ER. I feel bad about that, so...please let me help you?"

He couldn't argue with her reasoning. Except... "You didn't make me choose to do what I did. I could have just watched. I could have yelled to distract the cow. I didn't have to get in that pen. I didn't have to move to try to help you. So, you can let go of the guilt. No one had a gun pointed at my head. I chose to do what I did, and I'm facing the consequences. And I'm not angry or bitter about it, and I certainly don't blame you."

If anything, he'd been raised to face the consequences. To accept responsibility. To not sit around and point fingers at other people, whining and complaining that he hadn't been treated right.

He took what he got and dealt with it.

He supposed the hardest thing he'd had to do was to take what Blanche had dealt him and deal with it.

Mostly because he'd pledged his life to her, and she to him, and he thought that was the end of it. He thought they were routine.

Of course, he supposed, eventually, when he wasn't quite as angry and bitter or maybe quite so overwhelmed, he could look back and see if maybe there was something he'd done that had made her leave.

Maybe there was something or some things he needed to change about himself, even though she hadn't said.

She hadn't blamed him at all. She'd just said she was tired of boys and babies and constant work and had decided to go to the city and get a job. She wanted to be single again.

And that had been the end of that. She'd left and hadn't given her family a backward glance.

Chapter 3

Forget about the images in movies, TV shows and even many books (Jessie's being one of the exceptions) of being "in love" and finding a perspn that will "make" you always happy. It is a LIE and will never happen. Love -- true love -- is not a "feeling"; it is a CHOICE you need to make. Every day. Sometimes you may even need to make that choice every hour.

Or even minute by minute.
- W. Connolly from Pittsburgh, PA

G lory lay on the couch in the dark morning, listening to the soft sounds in the kitchen.

She'd checked her phone just a couple minutes ago, and it was 4:30. Armstrong had told her before she'd gone to the couch last night what time he usually got the kids up and what time the bus came.

He hadn't mentioned what time he'd be up to go feed. So, she didn't know whether he was right on time, or whether he was late.

She wanted to ask if he was okay, get up and make sure. There was just a part of her that felt responsible. He wouldn't be in the predicament he was in if it hadn't been for her breaking one of the first rules of working cattle: don't take your eyes off of the cow.

But she lay still. The blanket up to her chin, the pillow soft against her cheek.

He'd offered her his bed and said he'd sleep on the couch, but she couldn't do that. Not when he'd just come back from the hospital.

Not to mention, she didn't want to go into his room. It would feel weird.

She was fine on the couch and had slept solid for three hours.

But she was a light sleeper, and the soft noises in the kitchen had woken her up.

The door clicked, and she assumed Armstrong had gone out.

She had a few hours before she had to get the kids up, and he might even be in by then.

He had insisted that if she would take care of the children, he could do the chores.

She wasn't entirely sure about that, and she had protested a couple of times but then gave up.

If he didn't want help, she could accept that, and she wasn't going to push.

Still, she hated lying around while he was out in the cold, almost certainly in pain, working.

So, she got up and looked in the refrigerator to see if there was any breakfast food; he hadn't mentioned what they usually ate. She saw there were three eggs in a bowl, so she assumed he must have chickens somewhere, but there was no bacon or sausage.

Opening the freezer above the refrigerator, she found it was mostly empty.

Looking around, she opened a few cupboards and finally found some cereal.

Setting it out on the table, as well as some bowls with some spoons, and deciding to leave the milk in the refrigerator, she figured that was all the preparation she needed to do for breakfast, so she put her boots on and walked out.

There were lights on in the pole building that doubled as a barn, and she walked in the end door, moving through tractors and equipment, not seeing any sign of Armstrong, and on down to the end and through another door, which led into the stable area.

There must have been a bulb or two out, because the stable was not well lit, but she saw Armstrong not far away from the door, on his knees, one hand around his stomach, one hand on his pitchfork, his head bent, but his torso unnaturally straight.

Stubborn man.

She didn't say anything but walked over and pulled gently on the pitchfork.

His head jerked up, and then he winced, like any movement ripped him up.

"I think it would have been better if I'd come out to do the chores, and you'd stayed in to take care of the children." She hoped her words weren't coming out as too much of a rebuke. She didn't really mean it in that way, but she was sincere. He would have been better off staying inside. She wasn't sure whether he was on his knees by plan or by accident because he just couldn't stay up anymore, but regardless, he was obviously in a lot of pain.

"I can do it," he said, his words sounding low and calm and not really having any trace of the pain that he must be feeling. The pain that was written on his face.

"I'm sure you can. But I can do it without pain, which is, not to rub it in, better." She tried for humor, lifting her brows and putting just a little emphasis on better.

Maybe his lips twitched; she couldn't really say.

He showed her where he was forking the hay from and pointed out the mom and baby he had penned up.

The calf looked like it'd been born premature, maybe, since it was much smaller than any calf she'd ever seen.

As she forked the hay, she said casually, "Was this a preemie?"

"One of three. It's the only one that made it."

"I see," she said, knowing it was kind of odd that he had the cow in the barn but now understanding why. Triplets were rare, and she'd never seen any.

By the time she was finished, he was on his feet.

"I couldn't wait to take pain pills until this morning, but they don't seem to be doing much of anything. And I know I can't get in the skid loader and roll hay out on the ground." It seemed to pain him to say it, mentally, almost more than physically.

"I've run skid loaders more than once in my life, I think I can handle it. You'll have to show me how to roll the hay."

"It's not hard."

They went back, and she got the skid loader out and listened while he explained to her what she needed to do once she got in the field.

"I can open the gate for you. I don't know where the cows are. Sometimes I drive till I find them, just to get an eyeball on them, but you don't have to do that. Just put it out wherever you think you can, and they'll come find it."

She nodded. She wasn't going to drive all over his property, not knowing where the boundary lines were, especially in the dark. Although, time had slipped by, and they only had half an hour until it was time to get the boys up for school.

She fed the hay without any trouble, all four bales, then brought the skid loader back to the barn. He was waiting at the gate, his head resting on the top of the post, but he straightened when he heard her coming and got it open for her to run through without having to stop.

He was moving slowly, like an old man, and she wished there were something she could do, but short of what she was doing, there wasn't anything since she couldn't take the pain from him.

When she had the skid loader shut off and parked in the shed, she climbed out and walked out to meet him as he slowly walked up.

"I just need to water still. That shouldn't be too hard. I can get it," he said. This time, his voice held a note of the pain she'd seen on his face earlier, and she figured he'd probably overdone it. While she hated to leave him, figuring she was just as likely to come out and see him passed out on the ground outside, it was time for the kids to get up.

"How soon do you think you'll be in?"

"On a good day, I can do it in twenty minutes, but today? Don't worry about me until the boys get on the bus."

"It'll be easier to take you to the hospital if you're not unconscious." She lifted a shoulder. "Just want to throw that out there."

"Thanks. I'll keep it in mind. If I feel like passing out, I'll resist the urge, just so I can make it easier on you."

There was a lot of sarcasm in his voice, but there was also the hint of a smile, which she hadn't seen the entire morning, despite the fact that his eyes were pinched and tight.

"Glad to see you can still laugh," she said. Even though he hadn't exactly laughed.

She turned without waiting for him to respond, thinking that if she had time before the kids got on the bus, she'd come out and check. It couldn't be good for him to be lying on the cold ground. The temperatures must be in the forties, although she hadn't checked, didn't know where his thermometer was. Her phone wasn't dependable outside of town.

After removing her boots and washing her hands, she walked upstairs.

At least she'd put the kids to bed, so she knew which rooms they were in.

Daniel had crawled out of his bed and was sleeping with Adam.

Otherwise, the boys were where she had left them.

Only now Caleb was in a room by himself, while Benjamin and Adam, along with the runaway Daniel, were all together in one room.

That would make it a little bit more complicated for her to wake them up without waking Daniel too.

She wasn't sure whether the little boys slept in past when the bigger boys did or not. When Armstrong had given his few terse sentences last night before they went to bed, he just mentioned getting the two boys up and on the bus.

She woke Benjamin first, with a finger to her lips as she pointed at Daniel.

He looked at his brother, and even though his face still had that confused sleepy look, he understood he needed to be quiet.

He looked at her again, like he was trying to place her, and she could almost see the memories coming back into his little brain.

Armstrong had said their clothes were in the dresser, so she rooted around until she found something that looked like it would fit and didn't have any holes in it. She figured they probably just wore T-shirts and jeans to school, so she didn't dress them in anything fancier but did add a sweatshirt because of the chill in the air.

It was a little trickier to wake Adam up, but she did that while Benjamin walked over to go to the bathroom.

Adam seemed to know before he even opened his eyes that Daniel was with him though, and she figured it must be a regular thing, because Adam was careful to move slowly and not wake his brother.

She had to admit she was impressed that he managed to get out of bed without waking Daniel.

She picked out clothes for him from the dresser on his side of the room and laid them at the foot of the bed.

Looking around, she found their sneakers and set them out too.

It probably wasn't too much for her to assume they could dress themselves.

At their age, she would expect it, especially since they'd been living with just a dad. He probably wasn't going to baby them like a mom might.

Adam had left the room, and she caught Benjamin on his way back, having left the door cracked so they wouldn't have to open it again.

"Can you get dressed by yourself?"

He nodded his head, rubbing one eye.

"Come on down when you're done, and I'll get you some cereal."

He nodded again and shuffled into his room.

All she had to do was make sure he didn't go back to bed.

Her little sister Orchid had been notorious for that. Their mom would get her out of bed, and as soon as her mom left the room, Orchid would crawl back under the covers.

She got disciplined for missing the bus multiple times during her elementary school years.

Even in high school, Orchid had always been the one to struggle getting up.

She was also the one that was wide awake at midnight.

Walking down the stairs, Glory surveyed the kitchen and then decided to tackle the dirty dishes in the sink while she waited for the boys.

They weren't piled up quite as high as she might have expected, for a man living alone with his kids, but there were still a lot of them nonetheless. And no dishwasher in sight.

Rolling her sleeves up, she drew some water and started washing.

Ten minutes had gone by, and she almost dried her hands off and walked back upstairs, when she heard footsteps on the stairs.

The two little boys came down, their faces still drowsy with sleep and one side of Adam's hair sticking straight up.

She hadn't even noticed that when he'd gotten out of bed, probably because she was so concerned about waking Daniel up, so she whispered, "Come on over here to the sink, and I'll put a little water in your hair. It's sticking up."

His little hand went to his head, almost like he was trying to figure out what in the world she was talking about. But he came over obediently, and she patted it down with some of her dishwater, wetting it until it didn't lay perfectly but was better than it had been.

"It looks like you guys have two kinds of cereal to pick from. I'll get the milk out."

They pulled out chairs and sat down, reaching for the cereal box without too much complaint or comment. Considering how talkative Adam had been before he'd gone to bed, he'd woken up almost the opposite.

It was probably a much later night than the boys were used to.

She didn't try to talk to them too much, just asked where their book bags were and if they had any homework.

She had no idea whether kids that age were getting homework or not. Although she couldn't ever remember bringing a book home other than to read throughout her elementary school years.

But the boys each had bags, and then she was getting ready to send them out the door when she gasped.

"Do you guys need lunches?"

"Oh. Yeah. Dad always makes us a sandwich."

She glanced at the time. Five minutes until the bus came.

The morning had been going so well too.

"What kind of sandwich does he usually make?" she asked, looking around for the bread.

"Peanut butter and jelly," Adam said, without any more commentary.

If Glory hadn't been in such a big rush to get the sandwiches made, she would have laughed at the difference. Last night if she'd have asked that question, Adam would have gone on for five minutes answering her.

Still, the peanut butter was where she expected it to be, and there was jelly in the refrigerator. Once she found the bread, she slapped two sandwiches together fairly quickly.

Grabbing a package of crackers that she'd found when she was looking for the bread, and an apple for each bag, she shoved them in their boxes and handed them over.

"There. And I don't think you've missed the bus."

"No. Sometimes she'll wait on us if she sees us coming," Adam said. Obviously he was starting to wake up.

"Well, let's get out the door so she sees you. And I hope you guys have a really great day." She wasn't sure about this next thing, but she did what she instinctively felt like she should do and leaned down, grabbing a boy in each arm and squeezing them to her.

They were sweet kids, had been obedient, and hadn't questioned her with anything. She wouldn't mind watching kids who acted like that.

From her teenage years and the little bit of babysitting she'd done when Rose hadn't been able to, she remembered the kids had been terrible, not listening, hard to control, and always into the things they shouldn't be.

It was almost enough to make her swear off ever wanting to have kids herself. And in fact, she really hadn't thought about it much.

She had thought more about having a romance, someone to love. But kids? Not so much.

Benjamin, Adam, Caleb, and Daniel could possibly change her mind.

"Tell Dad we said bye," Benjamin said.

Adam nodded. Like he hadn't thought of that but had been wondering where his dad was.

"I will. He was out feeding, just going a little slower today because he's a little bit sore."

That was an understatement, but the kids didn't notice, and she stood on the porch watching as they walked out to the end of the drive.

They'd just reached the end, standing beside the mailbox, when the bus came into sight.

It wasn't even light out, and she felt bad that they had to start their days so early.

The little boys got on, Benjamin turning around to wave to her before he disappeared inside, and the bus pulled away.

She felt strangely bereft, like she just sent away her own children instead of someone else's. An odd feeling, and she shook her head.

Sticking her head inside the house, making sure none of the other boys had come down the stairs, she figured she'd run over to the barn and check on Armstrong. He said that he'd be done by the time the kids got on the bus.

She didn't see anyone inside at all, so, saying a prayer that the worst hadn't happened, she jogged across the yard.

Chapter 4

Make Jesus the center of your marriage. Love your spouse as Jesus loves you, along with lots of forgiveness and a never give up attitude.
- Dora from Virginia

G lory leaned the bulky box against the church wall, balancing it on her leg, as she reached to open the door with her other hand.

Armstrong had walked out of the door just as she reached the barn this morning for the second time.

He had been fine, if looking a little weak and white and tense.

His arm had been completely out of his sleeve, and his hand hugged his stomach under his coat.

Still, he assured her that he was fine, thanked her, and told her she could leave.

On the way, Miss Charlene from church had texted her and asked her if she would stop at the post office and pick up a box for the Piece Makers' meeting later.

Miss Charlene had neglected to mention that the box was almost as big as she was, although she supposed it was better for her to do it than it was for the ladies to try to wrestle it around.

It was probably material, although she didn't know.

Regardless, Glory walked into the church, kicking the door shut behind her, peeking over the top of the box to make sure she didn't run into anything as she walked across the floor and set it on the side table.

"Goodness! I wasn't expecting a box that big," Miss Charlene said, standing up and coming over to Glory.

"I wasn't either. When you said box, I thought I would be able to carry it, you know, with one hand."

"We ordered a lot of material this month. We actually made more quilts last month than we ever have in a month before." Miss Vicky waved at her from the quilting frame she sat in front of.

Kathy sat on the other side, and they pushed the needle back and forth. Glory didn't know much about quilting, and she wasn't sure exactly what they were doing, but it looked complicated.

"We heard you had some excitement at the sale barn last night," Charlene said, walking back over to the table in a slow, casual manner that invited Glory to walk along beside her.

Kathy was sitting at the table and looked up as Glory stopped in front of her. "We heard Armstrong Brandt from north of town ended up in the ER, and because of you," she said, looking at Glory over the top of her glasses, similar to the way a serious schoolmarm might. Glory almost felt like she was in trouble.

The guilt she felt that Armstrong had gotten laid up because of her came back full force.

"You heard right. I wasn't paying attention and got chased by a mama cow. He jumped in to save me and ended up getting hurt. He said he had three cracked ribs."

Charlene snapped her head over at the idea of three cracked ribs.

"She got him good," she said, concern lacing her tone.

"Yeah. She did. And like I said, it was my fault."

"Don't be too hard on yourself. Accidents happen, and he didn't have to jump in there to save you. Not to mention, my source told me that you rushed to save him when he was down. You drew the cow to you so he could get up." Charlene put a gentle hand on the small of Glory's back, and it felt as comforting as a big bear hug.

"I guess that's true. I did." But it seemed like too little, too late.

"Well, if you have a few minutes, would you sit down, because we have something we need to ask you," Charlene said, waiting for Glory to look at her, surprised, before she walked to the end of the table and pulled her chair out.

Her mom was expecting her at the sale barn, because several people hadn't been able to take their animals home last night and were coming to load them at dinnertime today.

She would be expected to help with that, and then there was the paperwork that needed to be done. That was her least favorite job, but a necessity, and she wouldn't complain because she had lots of fun things that she got to do. A little paperwork wasn't going to upset her equilibrium.

"Can I help you guys do something?" she asked, figuring that that was probably what they wanted.

They were somewhat known for their matchmaking in town, or maybe somewhat notorious for it, since they tried to match her mother with Mr. Powers. Which had been an unmitigated disaster.

It would be legend in Sweet Water for years to come.

She was pretty sure that the ladies had gotten out of their matchmaking urges, although she supposed they had kind of done something with her sister Marigold. Marigold had been vague on the details of how the Piece Makers had been involved.

Regardless, living in a small town meant lending a hand to whoever needed it, whenever she could.

Because she was single, and because her job had flexible hours, Glory had time to help, and she was young and spry and could do it. So she figured whatever they asked her to do, she'd help them. Whether it was quilting or cleaning out their attics or cellars.

"We've already talked about Armstrong and what happened to him yesterday, so this probably makes it even more necessary," Charlene began, and Glory tried not to flinch.

She couldn't seem to get away from the man. And she had to admit she admired him.

He was like a lot of other farmers, who would work through the pain, but he also had four children, and they'd obviously been well taken care of. Disciplined and corrected, well fed, and the house was neat, set up for children.

She'd been impressed.

Whatever had happened in their marriage, he definitely had been focused on taking care of his children. Which couldn't be easy as he tried to work his farm as well.

It would take a man with a lot of strength of character, which often translated into someone who might be stubborn and commanding as well.

Maybe that was hard for his wife to live with.

She didn't want to speculate.

"Yeah?" she said, when Charlene seemed to be waiting for her to respond.

"The whole reason he was here yesterday was because he was asking around to see if someone would be able to watch his kids for the summer, and even now, after school, while he tries to get the spring work done."

Glory still didn't think they were talking about her. Maybe they wanted her to find someone, or maybe they were going to ask if one of her sisters would be willing.

Rose was great with kids, but she was married and busy with her new husband. But she'd probably be willing to watch the four kids if Armstrong would bring them to her house every day.

Glory doubted Armstrong would want to do that; that was an hour and a half of driving before he even could start on his work. Then an hour and a half to pick them up. Three hours of his day gone.

Yeah, that probably wasn't going to happen.

"Did he find someone?" she asked, since Charlene seemed to be waiting for her again.

"We were thinking of you."

"Me?" She sat up. True, she didn't have anything but the sale barn planned for this summer. Her mom had just hired someone to take Rose's place, because of Rose's marriage.

So as long as that person worked out, she probably had some flexibility in her schedule.

"I'm not very good with kids," she said finally. Although his boys hadn't been hard to deal with.

"You're great with kids. I've seen you in junior church. You have Rose as your example, and she's like a prodigy with children."

"Yeah." That was a good way of looking at Rose's abilities.

"Well, we figured," Charlene's look had gotten sly, "it was your fault that he was laid up, and since he'll need someone even worse than what he thought he would because of that, we would check with you first. It's just for the summer." Charlene glanced over at Kathy, and a look flashed between them.

Glory wasn't sure exactly what that meant, but she kinda figured it didn't really matter.

Charlene had just played her trump card. She hadn't even waited until the end of the conversation to lay it down.

Glory could hardly deny her now.

"You have his number?" she asked, not nearly as reluctant as what she thought she should be.

She didn't really want to be tied down all summer watching kids. And she didn't really want to be out of Sweet Water, forty minutes away from everyone she knew.

But it was true that she really didn't have any other plans, and it was also true that...she felt a strange admiration for Armstrong.

Was admiration the right word?

Her brain wanted to insert attraction, but she didn't want to allow that word to be used.

She definitely didn't want to admit to being attracted to him.

That would be awkward if she had to work with him all summer. Especially since he was obviously not attracted to her.

He might have been in pain every time he had spoken to her, but the fact of the matter was he just didn't seem to like her very much.

Charlene smiled like she just won a hundred bucks in poker. "Yes. He left it yesterday, when he stopped in. It's at the diner and has been going around town."

She pulled her phone out and scrolled through a couple of texts before she read the number off to Glory.

"I have to let a few people know that we have it covered. There's nothing like a handsome man in town asking around for help to get the ladies stirred up," Vicki added.

That was the truth. It was funny how a man could get ladies to run to his beck and call a lot faster than a lady could get ladies to do the same thing.

It was funny how ladies were kind of sexist against themselves, and she didn't even really think they realized it.

"So am I just supposed to call and volunteer? Did he leave any information about it?"

"He preferred someone who would live at his house. But I suppose if you want to drive back and forth, that would be up to you. He shouldn't need anyone for at night, although with his broken ribs..." Charlene let the sentence dangle right there, right in front of Glory's face, right there were she could see her guilt, feel it pinching her neck, pulling in her stomach, reminding her that the man had a farm to run, and now he was going to do it through a haze of pain for the next month or two, and all because of her.

"I could probably do that." She wasn't super eager to do it. There were four children who would act as chaperones, but staying overnight at a single man's house had never been something that she'd ever really wanted to do. It gave the wrong impression for sure.

But if the whole town knew she was working...people would still talk anyway, but maybe she and Armstrong could come up with something that would work.

She supposed she could handle a few rumors, if he could handle a lot of pain.

"I'll give him a call, and I'll tell him I'll do it," she said, almost, for some strange reason, looking forward to it.

The ladies just smiled, and Charlene said, "I thought we could count on you." She looked around at the other ladies. "You can call now if you want to, but that's all we wanted to talk to you about. And thanks for bringing the box."

Glory stood. She loved the ladies, but she thought this might be a phone call she wanted to have in private.

"You know my number if you need anything," she said, and she didn't add anything to that, knowing that the ladies would not be afraid to use it if they wanted her.

Chapter 5

Friendship with lots of humor.
- Sheila Bryant from SC

"Will you lay down with me for a minute?" Caleb's sleepy voice said from underneath a thick blanket where Armstrong was tucking him in.

His ribs ached, a sharp pain every time he moved, and he wanted to lie down, but he needed to get something out for supper, and he wanted to check the stock while the boys were sleeping.

Normally he did that while they were with him, carrying one on his shoulders and sometimes one on his back. At the very least, holding their hands and swinging them.

He tried to make it fun for the kids, because he couldn't stand the idea of going out and doing work and having it be drudgery for him every day. So, maybe it was just as much for him as it was for the boys.

He loved it. There wasn't anything else he'd rather do. But with the way his ribs felt, he knew he couldn't carry anyone, and swinging his arms was out of the question.

"I'm sorry, but not today." He leaned down, holding his breath against the pain as he put his lips on his son's forehead.

He'd already kissed Daniel, and Daniel had his thumb in his mouth, his hand under his cheek, his eyes on his dad.

Sometimes the boys didn't take a nap. Sometimes he sat in his easy chair with them on his lap, snuggled up to him, and they all took a nap together.

That was often what they did in winters when the afternoons were cold and dark.

Not today.

His phone buzzed in his pocket, and he gave them one last glance before he slipped out of the room, closing the door quietly and pulling his phone out of his pocket.

It was a number he didn't recognize.

Lord, please let it be someone who can give me a hand with the kids and let them be on their way right now.

His kids were his main concern, even though the wrapping around his chest was going to need to be changed if he took a shower tonight. He supposed he could go a couple of days without showering, and the kids wouldn't complain, since the tightness around his chest made the pain at least bearable.

It had hurt like everything to put it on, and he was guessing it would hurt even worse to take it off, but he really wanted to wear it, because the support was invaluable.

Lord?

Maybe when he went into town to pick up his prescription, he should have asked around to see if someone was willing to help him change his bandage once a day.

Normally he didn't find watching his children a chore. It was hard to get farm work done, but as much as he could, he took them with him. Just four was too many to ride the tractor at one time.

He didn't want them to be neglected all summer, so he needed help.

Swiping, he said, "Hello?"

"Armstrong?" a soft feminine voice said on the other end.

It sounded an awful lot like...Glory.

He didn't want to think about her though. She'd seen him at his worst.

She hadn't batted an eye. Of course, she had been working from a place of guilt, which irritated him. He didn't want her to be here because she felt guilty that he was laid up.

But she dug into the farm work, dug into the kids, dug in and did the dishes even. She'd slept on the couch, just thrown in with whatever needed to be done.

Maybe, maybe if he were looking for a wife, that would be the kind of wife he'd want.

But after what he'd been through, he certainly wasn't looking.

"It's Glory Baldwin. I was just there this morning?"

Like he could forget. Like he didn't know who she was.

Like she normally had men forget her. She probably went out with someone different every week.

And he had four children. They were in different stages of their life, and he needed to remember that.

When he was single and unattached, a woman with four kids was not someone he looked twice at.

"I know who you are," he said, knowing his words were abrupt but wanting her to get to the point. He didn't need her melodious voice in his ear to remind him of all the mistakes that he'd made. All the things he didn't have. All the things he needed right now.

"The Piece Maker ladies said that you're looking for someone to watch your children. I was wondering if you would consider me?"

He stopped, right in the middle of his kitchen floor. The phone held to his ear, but his mouth open. Surprise almost making him forget about the pain that had been his constant companion since his ribs had been smashed.

Was that coincidence? He had just prayed. He'd just asked for someone, and the phone had rung.

God, I wish you answered every prayer like that. Kinda makes me suspicious when it happens out of the blue.

He hated to look a gift horse in the mouth, and he hated to question God over how he was going to answer a prayer, but really? The woman he was just thinking about calls and offers.

"I know you feel guilty. You don't have to."

"It's not because I feel guilty. Charlene actually asked me if I would do it. I guess I was the one she was thinking of, even before last night."

"You looking for a job?"

"I work at the auction barn. We'd have to figure out a schedule around that, because I might be able to get out of the things that we do during the week, but I know I won't be able to get out of the auction, especially in the summer when we're busy."

"They're Wednesdays and Saturdays, right?"

"Yeah."

"We can work around that." What was he saying? Had he accepted her offer? He didn't want to accept her offer. He didn't want her here. Except...he did.

"When can I start? I know you need someone, and I'm willing anytime. I've already talked with my mom, and she just hired someone, and they're in good shape." She took a breath. "Maybe sometimes things would come up, but I might be able to take at least two of the boys with me, if you can handle the other two. Not all the time."

"No. I get it. It was gonna involve some housework as well. And..." Could he ask her to help him with the feeding and the barn work?

He hated to. But the idea of riding in a skid loader was more than he could bear right now.

"I guess we can talk about it whenever you get here. I assume you're staying?"

"Well, I can." She didn't seem too sure about that, and he figured it was because he was a single man living alone with his kids.

"There's a spare bedroom upstairs. Or you can have the couch. But it's fine if you want to leave at a certain time every night and get here at a certain time every morning. That's just a long drive."

"I know. And I'm sure there will be times this summer where you're working late, and it will be a late drive too. If you don't mind, I'll stay."

"That's great. I'll see you when you get here, and we'll figure out what your jobs are."

He hadn't even made a list. He just needed someone to watch the kids, maybe get groceries, do a little cleaning and dishes and that type of thing. But now...now he might end up watching the children, because he knew she could handle the feeding. She knew her way around the barn.

He saw a truck pulling into the drive, so he went ahead and walked out on the porch in his stocking feet.

Normally he might sit on the top step or lean against the porch railing or post, but standing seemed to be the least painful position, so that's what he did.

He didn't recognize the truck, but as soon as the man got out, he recognized Coleman, who was Glory's brother and the manager at the sale barn.

He was probably coming out to make sure Armstrong wasn't going to sue.

As if.

Coleman walked to the bottom of the porch stairs.

"You're up anyway," he said in greeting.

"The cows weren't going to feed themselves this morning. Although, the grass is growing, and pretty soon they will."

If this had happened just a few weeks later, the grass really would be growing and he wouldn't need to supplement with hay at all.

"Bad timing, with the spring work right around the corner."

"I know. But if God hadn't wanted me to break my ribs, he could have kept it from happening, so it might be bad timing on my end but perfect timing on God's."

"Good way of looking at it. Can't change it for sure," Coleman said, nodding and putting one foot up on the second step and leaning a forearm on it. "Somebody would have been out to help you last night, but I knew Glory was here. She's practical and can do everything I can do, unless it takes brute strength." Coleman looked up, and his eyes narrowed a little, but he was just making conversation. "Orchid, on the other hand, would have been day-dreaming, and I wouldn't have known for sure whether she actually even would watch the kids let alone help you."

He assumed Orchid was the name of one of his other sisters. That was some kind of flower, although Armstrong couldn't picture it in his head. He wasn't even sure he'd ever seen an orchid.

"She was a great help. I had fed everything last night before I left, but she helped me this morning. The idea of riding in a skid loader right now makes me want to lie down and cry."

Coleman grinned a little. His face still looked serious even with a grin on it, which would seem to be quite an accomplishment. Not everybody could pull that look off.

Not everybody would want to try.

"Yeah. Glory can take things in hand and isn't shy. But I know she's back in town, because I passed her at the post office, so I figured I'd come out and see if there was anything I can do."

"Actually, I just got off the phone with Glory. I'm hiring her to watch the kids." Armstrong knew that Coleman and Glory's father had passed away a decade or more ago. Coleman was the head of the family, although he believed the mom called the shots. Regardless, if anybody was going to have a problem with him having Glory out at his place, it was going to be Coleman. He figured he might as well throw it out there, right now, before Glory even showed up. That way, if Coleman had issues, they quit before they even started.

Coleman nodded thoughtfully. "She's staying here?"

"Said she was," Armstrong said, leaving the implication that he had given her the choice of going home. He had, and she chose not to.

Coleman nodded. "I can't imagine that she'd be super thrilled about that, but I know she'll be a good help to you. Actually, as long she's here, you're not going to need anyone else. I was actually getting a crew together to take turns coming out to give you a hand. But if you've got Glory in your corner, you won't need us."

That was some pretty high confidence, and coming from Coleman, it was high praise indeed.

He hadn't misjudged Glory at all. In fact, if anything, he'd underestimated her.

"She's supposed to be on her way out, and we are going to talk about what I was expecting, which, honestly, I don't even know what I am."

"That's a little different today than it was yesterday." Coleman glanced at his ribs, and his look was telling. "But Glory's up to it. I don't think you could have anyone better." He looked around. "Is there anything you need me to do while I'm here?"

"No." There was a lot of stuff he could be doing, but nothing that was urgent.

"You need anything from town? Glory can bring it out with her."

"No. I ran in this morning and picked up my pain prescription, and that's pretty much it."

He supposed Glory could probably go grocery shopping for him, and maybe she'd even make the list. He didn't know what she could cook. He hadn't been able to cook much of anything before his wife left. But he figured things out, with four hungry children bouncing around him while he held his phone up and tried to read recipes off of it since he didn't have a cookbook in the house.

They had survived.

"Thanks. I really appreciate you coming out here and checking up on me," he said. Knowing that probably there was some concerns about a lawsuit, but Coleman hadn't said anything about it, and he figured he wouldn't. It was the neighborly thing to do, and he was guessing that that was the main reason Coleman was here.

Coleman shrugged off his thanks. "If you need anything, let me know. Tell Glory. She's not afraid to ask." He looked a lot like an older brother who might tweak his little sister's nose, if she'd been standing there. "I'm not going to hang out here. If you've got her coming, you don't need me."

"No. Go on."

Coleman jerked his head again, then turned and walked to his pickup, getting in and driving away. He'd probably meet his sister on her way out, but in the meantime, Armstrong needed to figure out what he was going to ask her to do. Probably make a list. That would be a good idea.

Maybe that would take his mind off his ribs, which seemed to be hurting worse now than they had been this morning.

Grimacing, wondering how long until the pain would fade away, he walked slowly into the house.

Chapter 6

Communication, get the help you need, and don't get divorced. Came close many years ago, 41 years strong.
- Susan Seibel

G lory knocked on the door, twisting the knob and pushing it open. She didn't want to make Armstrong have to answer. Especially since she could hear noises inside like the kids were up and things were happening.

"Mornin'," Armstrong said from the floor where he knelt with one knee down, his face contorted, as Daniel lay on the ground, his diaper half off.

It was obvious that he was trying to change the diaper with one hand while holding his ribs with the other.

"When you left the hospital, did they tell you to stay in bed?" she asked, figuring he most definitely wasn't supposed to be doing what he was doing.

He gave her a dark look, and didn't respond, but put two fingers on the diaper, and used his thumb and first finger to try to pull the tab off.

She didn't want to be bossy, and she didn't want to be mothering, but the poor kid was never going to get his diaper changed if he lay around waiting for his dad to try to figure out how to get it done with one hand.

Without saying anything, Glory walked over, knelt down, and pulled both tabs of the diaper off. Thankfully it was just wet.

She set the dirty diaper aside and held her hand out for the clean one.

Daniel looked at her calmly, like two people changed his diaper all the time, or maybe he was just fine since he'd spent so much time with her at the auction the night before.

It would have made it awkward if Daniel were throwing a fit, but since he didn't, it was easy for her to take over without scolding Armstrong like he was a little child.

Sticking the new diaper on and grateful for all the kids that Rose had babysat over the years and needed help with, since she was somewhat adept at changing diapers, she stood him up and said to him, "Where are your pants?"

His little shoulder shrugged up and down, and she looked at Armstrong.

The corners of his mouth were white, and there were pain lines between his brows.

"I didn't get pants. It was all I could do to get the diaper. He wants me to hold him, and...I just can't."

"I know. It must be so frustrating not to do what you're used to being able to do. But I think... I know you don't want to hear it, but the easier you are on yourself now, the faster those ribs will heal. It's going to take longer if you keep moving them so they can't set."

She wasn't sure whether that was the correct medical terminology or not, but she did know that if he didn't take it easy, they wouldn't heal as fast.

"I know. You're right." He looked a little green, and his words seemed to be pulled out of him.

She stood, but he'd stayed on the ground.

"Are you going to throw up?" She asked the first question that popped in her head since his stance put her in mind of someone who was sick to their stomach, probably from the pain.

"I'm trying not to," he said, swallowing hard.

"Daddy hurts," Caleb said seriously, standing beside the chair, looking at her with big eyes.

"I know. It's my fault Daddy hurts."

"Stop that," he snapped, more forcefully than maybe he would have if he weren't hurting so bad.

"It's the truth."

"It's really not. I didn't do anything I didn't choose to do. Stop blaming yourself. I don't want to focus on feeling sick and hurting. So we're not going to talk about that anymore."

She looked at him, her head tilted. Did he just make a joke?

She huffed out a breath, and he looked up at her, humor in his eyes although his mouth tightened and the pain lines were worse. He also was some shade of color between death gray and puke green.

"If I quit talking about it, you'll go lay down?"

He snorted a little, which came out in a painful half grunt, half laugh. "I can't move right now. Or I would."

"I'd suggest you lie down on the floor, but...I think that would hurt even worse."

"Yeah. That makes it worse just thinking about it."

"Sorry."

"No more apologizing for the rest of the day," he said shortly.

"I'll try. Feels like I should help you somehow, but I think maybe I'll just take the boys and we'll start working on supper, and I'll let you try to figure out how to get up from the floor yourself."

"Thanks. I knew I could count on you."

She laughed again. She liked that he was on the floor, couldn't get up, was in so much pain he thought he was gonna throw up, and he was laughing and being sarcastic.

In her experience, when men were helpless, they often got angry. She liked that it wasn't his default. Or maybe he'd made it so it wasn't.

Maybe having children had tempered him some.

Whatever it was, she appreciated it.

"How about it, boys? You guys going to help me cook?"

She reached down, picking Daniel up, and saw Caleb's serious face nodding up and down.

"First though, we need to get some pants on this kid. He can hardly cook supper with his bare legs sticking out." She leaned over a little and looked at Caleb. "Do you think you can help me find some pants for him?"

Caleb's head went up and down again, very seriously.

"Will you hold my hand and take me to them?" she asked.

He reached out and took a hold of her hand, leading her to the stairs and starting up them.

Tempted to look back to see how Armstrong was doing, she didn't. He was a man, and he wanted to do it himself. She couldn't imagine that his ribs would feel any better if she gave him a hand up. It was going to hurt no matter what, and at least this way, she'd be taking care of the children and he wouldn't have an audience.

She didn't know what she was going to do if he couldn't get up. Her brain teased that thought in the back of her head, and she shoved it aside.

If he was still on the floor when she came back down, she'd have to figure something out. Or else, maybe he just wanted her to leave him there.

She chattered with the boys as Caleb showed her where Daniel's pants were, and she kinda laughed at the fact that they weren't folded.

At least they were in a drawer.

Whether it was Armstrong who did the laundry, or whether one of the boys had helped him put them away, it made sense to her that if they were going to skip a step, they'd skip the folding.

Nobody was going to care if the baby's pants were wrinkled.

She supposed seeing clothes put in a drawer but not folded would give some ladies the vapors. She actually thought it might be something she could implement in her own routine. Nobody cared if her jeans were folded after all.

With Daniel properly dressed, she brought the boys back down the stairs, and thankfully, Armstrong was no longer on the floor.

As they walked by the opening to the living room, she glanced in, and he seemed to be uncomfortably perched on his back, half leaning against the back of the sofa, his face scrunched up.

"Hang on a second, boys. Let's see if your dad needs anything before we start."

She needed to carry the rest of the groceries that she'd gotten them from her car, but she stood in the doorway. "Do you need pain pills?"

"Do you mind? I was going to get them, but...it was all I could do to make it to the couch."

"No. I understand, and I think you're smart. I think once the pain gets ahead of you, it's hard to get a hold of it again."

"Now you tell me."

She snorted. "I'm sure they probably told you that in the ER."

"I didn't hear it."

She rolled her eyes but let that go. He probably didn't hear it because he didn't want to or didn't believe them. Or was so focused on getting out of there that he didn't care what they were saying.

"Where are they?" she asked.

"On the fridge. I didn't want the boys to get them in case something happened to me." His voice sounded weaker but still pain laced.

"I'm going to set you down for a minute, okay, bud?" she said to Daniel, who didn't look very happy about the idea but didn't fuss when she set him on the ground.

She grabbed the bottle with the name of the medication that he mentioned on it and then went to the sink, grabbing a glass and letting the cold water run for a bit before she filled it.

The boys trailed after her as she walked in. How was Armstrong going to sit up enough to take the medication? Any way he moved had to hurt.

He grimaced, but rolled over a little bit, and threw the pills in his mouth, chugging several big gulps of water before handing the glass back to her and resting back on the couch with a sigh of relief.

From his position, she doubted the pain was completely gone, but maybe it didn't feel quite as bad.

"The boys should be home from school anytime," he said wearily.

"I'll work on supper, and if you let me know what needs to be done with the animals this evening, I'll make sure that gets done if I can leave Caleb and Daniel in here with you."

"I usually take them with me, but it'll probably be easier without them."

"Maybe not. Maybe they can tell me what to do." She figured it might just be better for him to not have to worry about them. Maybe he'd fall asleep.

She wished he were upstairs in his bedroom so she wouldn't have to worry about keeping the children quiet all afternoon and evening, if he did.

She thought about suggesting he go up but decided against it. He probably already felt useless enough and wouldn't want to be completely out of the picture if anything happened and he were needed.

"Come on, boys. I have some more groceries out in the car. We can set what I already brought in on the table, then we'll go get some more."

"Can I help?" Caleb asked, still serious, but something that looked like hope had entered his eyes.

She smiled at him, and although he didn't smile back, his head lowered a little, like he was a bit embarrassed by her attention.

"I'd really like it if you could help me. That will save me a couple of trips. You look like you're pretty strong,"

His chest puffed out a little, and he looked at her from under his lashes.

Armstrong seemed to have done an excellent job with his children, but it had to have affected them to have their mom walk out, and even though no one had probably told the kids she didn't want them, kids were often very astute and didn't need someone to spell things out for them to come to the right conclusions.

With that in mind, it was easy to be patient with the boys as they "helped" her get supper ready. When Benjamin and Adam got off school, they were eager to go out and help, and the four of them did the feeding with her.

Adam had a little bit of homework, which he finished after supper. Armstrong was snoring, and she didn't want to wake him to bring him to the table, so the kids and she ate without him.

It was nice enough outside that after supper they went out and ran around some before she brought the boys in, gave the two little ones baths, and had the older two shower themselves, and then she read to them for a while before bed.

Armstrong woke up just as she was about to shut her book and tell the boys it was bedtime.

She had explained to the boys while they were outside that they had to be careful with their dad, gentle with him, and they seemed to remember as they walked gingerly over to the couch and stood back, three of the boys with their hands behind their backs, Daniel with his clasped in front of him, careful not to touch their dad.

Glory smiled at the sweet little boys and how cute they were. How careful they were with their dad.

Armstrong noticed their odd positions and lifted a brow at her, even though the tight white skin around his eyes said that he was in just as much pain as he had been before.

The boys all said good night to him, and she shooed them up the stairs, turning to look back over her shoulder. "I brought my stuff in earlier, and it looked like there was a spare bed in Caleb and Daniel's room, so if it's okay, that's where I'm going to sleep."

"There's an empty bedroom up there. I was going to look to see if it needed to be cleaned but didn't get to it."

"I didn't want to take it." She hadn't been sure if maybe he had company coming at times or something else. It looked like there was a brush on the dresser and clothes in the closet.

"You have it." His voice sounded a little gravelly, the shadow on his face looking more like a beard than scruff.

"Thanks. I could have done it today." But she wasn't going to get to it now.

"I need to go out and check the stock."

"Okay. Take your phone, and if there's anything I missed or that needs to be done, give me a call. I'll go out and give you a hand at the very least."

He jerked his chin at her but didn't say anything. She guessed that if there was anything that needed to be done, the stubborn man would try to do it himself before he'd ask her for help.

"That's why I'm here. Remember? You'll get better faster if you let me help."

His lips moved a little, one side pulling back, and he jerked his head again but didn't look back at her as he moved slowly, painfully, to the door.

She turned her back on him and walked up the stairs, shaking her head. Stubborn man.

Chapter 7

If you're married in the church, you make vows before God,
which are not to be taken lightly. So many people approach
marriage these days with the attitude that if they don't like it,
or it doesn't work out, they can press the eject button and try
again with someone else. But those vows MEAN something.
They mean EVERYTHING. They bind you together for life.
I'm not saying a person should stay in an abusive or repeat-
edly adulterous situation. But marriage is hard. It's hard
work, and you're going to disagree, make each other mad, and
sometimes make some really big mistakes! Remember those
vows. Pray for your spouse daily, even when you don't feel like
it (especially when you don't feel like it!). Never stop talking to
each other, and ask the Lord for strength and guidance when
it gets hard.
– Alison Nye Winnipeg from Manitoba, Canada

Armstrong stood at the corral fence, his hands at his sides, which seemed to be the least painful position, not leaning on the fence but looking in at the few animals who stood there as the sun went down over the western horizon.

Glory had done the same thing today that she'd done yesterday and the day before.

She pretty much had everything in hand. The kids, the house, the meals, the laundry, and all the work outside. She made it look easy, and he wondered why he'd struggled even back before he'd gotten hurt.

The boys seemed to really enjoy her; they definitely enjoyed her stories and her reading to them at night. She made sure they did their schoolwork, and he couldn't fault her for anything.

Kind of annoyed him.

She was too perfect. And he was...stinky.

He hadn't showered since he broke his ribs, because he didn't know how to get the wrap off of his chest.

Actually, he was pretty sure he could get the wrap off, he just wasn't sure if he could get it back on, and the idea of living without it was painful.

So, he'd stayed away from her as much as he could this evening, moving away when she moved toward him and going outside after he'd hugged his children rather than going upstairs with her.

That almost killed him, because he wanted to be with his boys, and while he was still in a lot of pain, it didn't hurt nearly as bad as it had.

At least he didn't feel like he was going to throw up every time he moved.

Of course, he was taking the pain pills more regularly as well and not letting the pain get ahead of him. He'd learned his lesson there.

That first night had been a killer.

Especially since he picked Daniel up without thinking from his nap and almost dropped his son, and then while he was struggling to try to figure out what to do, Caleb had plowed into him like he always did and knocked him off balance and into the side of the crib.

He'd never been in that much pain.

That was what the biggest problem had been when Glory had walked in and found him with Daniel on the floor trying to change his diaper.

He hated looking weak in front of her. Hated having her be so perfect and him so...incompetent.

While at the same time, he appreciated her competence, appreciated her care with the children, couldn't imagine having someone, anyone else, taking care of his kids.

She did it better than he did.

She was even planning on going to the end-of-the-year field day next Tuesday with them.

She'd asked him first, of course, and he hadn't been sure if he would be up to spending an entire day on his feet.

He definitely wouldn't be up to having Caleb and Daniel, since Daniel would want to be carried around a good bit, and it was still extremely painful to pick him up.

But that was next week. Tonight, he had to figure out how to shower himself and get his wrap back on.

Glory would help you.

He didn't want her to. Didn't want to be so weak in front of her. Wasn't sure that he would be able to stand up without the wrap on, let alone take a shower, and he didn't want her to see that.

He stayed outside as long as he could. The cold didn't bother him, but the pain got to him and forced him back in, even though it hurt to sit almost as much as to stand. Maybe more.

Usually when Glory went upstairs, she didn't come back down but went to her room and stayed there for the evening. Whether to give him privacy or whether to get away from him, he wasn't sure and hadn't asked.

Mostly he didn't want to know.

Before he'd been married, before he had children, Glory would have been the kind of girl he would have been interested in.

But he couldn't afford to make the kind of mistake that he'd already made again.

Once was enough for a lifetime.

So, he was a little shocked when he opened the door and she was standing with her back to him at the counter, chopping vegetables or something.

She lifted her head but didn't turn the whole way around. "To-morrow is auction day, and I don't want to leave you with more than you can handle, but my family depends on me to give them a hand." She lifted a shoulder and looked back at what she was doing. "So I'm getting stuff ready right now, and I'll throw it in the crockpot in the morning. I'll get everything done that I can, but I'll probably leave around three or so, unless you have a major problem with it?"

She looked back as he shut the door and tried to walk with confidence through the kitchen, but if he were honest, his walk was more of a shuffle.

He was past due for a pain pill and should have come in half an hour ago and taken it.

Instead of being stubborn.

"Whatever you need to do. I don't want to keep you from your responsibilities," he said, and even though his voice was a little pinched, he thought it came out gently, all things considered.

But her head came up and she stopped and her whole body turned. "I don't have to go," she said, and there was a little bit of irritation in her voice, like he had been condescending to her.

"I'm sorry. That didn't come out the way I meant it. I just meant you have to do what you have to do, and I appreciate everything you've done. Everything. I couldn't ask for more, and..." He took a breath, blew it out, trying to blow his irritation out with it. "Maybe it's even a little annoying that you can do everything I do, and you can do it better."

"Because I don't have three broken ribs? Because I didn't save someone's life? Don't knock yourself up about it."

He didn't say anything more. She wouldn't understand. When a person's spouse walked out on them, it made them feel like a failure. Then, when they couldn't keep all the balls spinning, couldn't keep the laundry caught up, couldn't keep the farm chores done as well as they used to, couldn't process their grief, couldn't stand to see their children cry at night, couldn't do anything about it, couldn't figure out how to help them, any one of those things would make a person feel like a failure.

Having all of them happen? He'd always considered himself a pretty competent person, but it was a lot.

He went to the fridge, wincing as he reached out for the pain pills. Wondering for the millionth time how long this was going to last. Even taking it as easy as he could, his recovery was too slow, and Glory had made it easy.

"I don't want to push you, but if you want to take a shower tonight, I can help you with the wrap around your chest." She spoke casually, her back to him, sounding like she didn't give a flip whether he did it or not but was just throwing it out there.

He hadn't realized she'd noticed.

"Do I stink that bad?"

"My room is right beside the bathroom. It's the only bathroom in the house. I happen to know that you haven't been in it to shower. Just because I live beside it. I'm sorry if you think that's too nosy."

He almost grunted a laugh. "You didn't answer my question."

"You haven't bathed for three days. I'm pretty sure you probably do stink."

That still wasn't a solid answer. But he wasn't going to push. After all, he didn't really want her saying, "Yes, Armstrong, you smell like a hogpen, only worse."

He twisted the cap off, grimacing, tapping two pills in his hand.

He screwed the lid back on and put the bottle up, tempted to take the pills without any water so he wouldn't have to walk by her, now that he pointed out he smelled rank.

He walked to the sink anyway.

She didn't say anything until he set the glass back down on the counter, empty.

"You didn't say whether or not you want my help, and I don't care what you smell like. After all, it can't be any worse than Daniel's dirty diapers." Her mouth curled up in a grin, and her eyes twinkled. But he didn't smile.

He didn't want to be compared to a three-year-old. And somehow, the comment irritated him. He wanted her to see him as a man. Competent, strong, capable.

Not stinking and dirty and incapable because he was too weak to take his wrap off and put it back on.

But if there was anything this injury had taught him, it was that his pride was a lot stronger than it should be, and he needed to swallow a good bit of it. After all, pride wasn't something a Christian was supposed to nurture. It seemed like God had orchestrated the events in his life to be such that his excessive amount of pride was front and center. After all, a man could hardly keep his pride when his wife walked out.

When he needed help bathing.

When he couldn't get himself off the floor.

So, he said, "I've put it off because I wasn't sure whether I would be able to or not. I appreciate your help."

He was getting ready to walk around her when she set the knife down with a clack and turned. Almost bumping into him.

"I thought you said you wanted my help?" she said when he looked at her in surprise.

He had. He just wasn't ready for it. Hadn't gotten to the point where his actions were following his thoughts and words.

When the nurses had put it on, he remembered specifically it had Velcro in the back.

If he walked away now, reaching around was going to hurt. If it wasn't impossible.

"You need help taking your shirt off?" she asked, like she did this every day.

He didn't say anything but just stood there, his hand reaching back, as he grimaced, trying to grab a fistful of his shirt behind him so he could pull it over his head. He could stand the pain to get his hand behind him, and he could even fist his shirt in his hand. But to pull the shirt over his head sent sharp blades of pain around his chest and down his torso. It wasn't enough to bring him to his knees, but only because he had them locked.

Waves of nausea rolled over him. He breathed through it.

She didn't say anything but stepped closer, grabbing her own fistfuls of the shirt, pulling it up, slipping it over his head, and pulling it down his arms which he held in front of him.

She threw the shirt on a chair and said, "I think it might start in the back."

She started to walk around, but he turned, giving her his back.

Her movements were gentle as she carefully pulled the Velcro off and began unwrapping.

It had been put on rather tightly, and he fought the lightheadedness as the wrap loosened and the support that he'd worn for three days slipped from his chest.

"Are you going to be okay?" she asked, concern in her tone.

He didn't answer. Really, he couldn't.

"Did they tell you anything in particular you needed to do when you took the wrap off?"

"No," he ground out. "I don't think they expected me to wear it for three days. I got used to it, like a crutch," he said, barely able to speak and breathe at the same time.

He sat down on the chair that she'd thrown his shirt on, just because he wasn't sure how much longer his legs would continue to hold him.

She didn't say anything, and he was grateful. He didn't want to have to answer a million questions.

She started busying herself doing something, and he suspected it was for him, so she wasn't just standing there staring at him, because he wasn't sure exactly what she was doing or if it was even necessary.

Regardless, he appreciated the fact that she didn't hover but just gave him covert glances, making sure he wasn't going to fall off the chair, apparently.

He almost laughed at that, but it was a legitimate concern. He himself wasn't sure he wasn't going to fall off the chair.

If it wouldn't have hurt him even worse, he would have put his head down on the table. But eventually the nausea passed, the weakness in his legs did too, and while the pain was still there, he got to the point where he felt like he could push through it.

So he did.

"Thanks," he said as he stood, fighting back the black spots that danced in front of his eyes. "I doubt I'll be in the shower long."

"Did they give you a new wrap, or should I see if we can reuse that one?" There was no disgust in her voice, like she was totally okay that she might have to reuse his dirty wrap.

"When I went to the pharmacy, I picked up enough for a week. Which was how long they told me I should keep it wrapped for. They're on the top of the refrigerator in the back."

Her eyes went to the refrigerator, and she jerked her head. "I'll be up in five minutes. Is that long enough?"

"Maybe a little longer, but not much." He took a breath and said it one more time, "Thanks."

Chapter 8

Never go to bed angry, stay calm when the other is mad or upset, kiss each other hello and goodbye, always say I Love You! Most of all; keep God in the relationship and talk to him often.
- Kelly Drewry from Collierville, TN

G lory stood in the kitchen, wiping her hands on a towel and trying to get her heart to stop clawing to get out of her chest.

In the summer, she saw men all the time without their shirts on around the auction barn.

Her mother frowned upon that, and usually people knew and respected her mom's preferences, but it wasn't like a man's chest was something she had never seen. Obviously.

But there'd been something about Armstrong standing in the kitchen, with no shirt on, that made it feel tight and small and like she couldn't breathe.

That should have been a completely unpleasant feeling, but it hadn't been.

She offered, because she knew if it were her, she would be dying to take a shower but probably wouldn't have wanted to ask for help. After all, she was an adult and had been taking a shower by herself for years. To all of the sudden need help and have to ask for it would be tough.

Men seemed to have even more difficulty with those kinds of things.

Regardless, somehow she needed to go upstairs, put a wrap on him, and try to pretend her hands weren't shaking, and also try to keep herself from doing anything but clinically doing her job.

It seemed like that might be more than she could handle.

Regardless, she grabbed a wrap from the bag on the top of the refrigerator and walked slowly up the stairs.

Hopefully, he would be able to get the bottom part of himself dressed before she needed to help.

She supposed, if she were a good caretaker, she would have made sure he was able to take care of himself like that, but it hadn't even occurred to her. She'd been so busy trying to make sure she was doing a good job with the children and the farm and the house that she hadn't thought to ask him about it.

The door to the bathroom opened when she was about ten feet away from it, walking down the hall.

Armstrong stood in the doorway, his face white, his jaw hard, his chest bare.

Thankfully, he had some kind of jogging pants on.

"I have it," she said, her voice sounding unnaturally high and cheerful.

She held up the wrap, like she needed to prove it. But silently she berated herself.

Relax. Why are you acting like a thirteen-year-old?

Maybe because she found Armstrong attractive from the first, but even though he thought she was just putting his wrap on, the same way a nurse would, she was having a hard time convincing herself that that's exactly what she was doing.

Suddenly she realized she'd been staring at his chest.

She looked at the corner of the hall, noting that there was a cobweb there. She'd have to get it tomorrow. She tried to focus on the cobweb, wondering what kind of spider might have made it.

It was a nice thought, but she was totally unsuccessful in getting her mind off the man standing in front of her.

Even spiders couldn't do that.

"Do you need me to sit down?" he asked slowly, probably wondering why in the world she was staring at the far corner.

Yep. In fact, he twisted a little, looking in the direction she was looking.

"No," she said quickly. She mentally beat her brain into submission. Focusing on the task at hand, kind of the way she did when she had an odious test to perform at the sale barn. A fractious cow, an angry bull, a flock of geese that wanted to go anywhere but where they were supposed to go.

Just jumped in and did what she had to do.

That's what she did now. Lifting her chin, she ripped the package open and strode forward.

"You're fine. Just hold your arms away from your sides as much as you can, and I'll do the rest."

There was no way she was going to be able to stand in front of him doing this, so she went around back behind him.

If he thought that was odd, he didn't say, but she felt justified in doing it because that's where she'd stood when she took it off.

She should have been concentrating more on him. How he must feel. He was probably desperate to sit down, because his skin seemed to tremble a little as she put her arms around him, meeting in front and pulling on the wrap, bringing it around both sides.

"Please tell me if I hurt you, or if I'm not doing it tight enough." Her voice was low in the stillness of the home, quiet because she didn't want to wake the children, but she forced it to not tremble. And was mostly successful.

"We can't put it too tight." His words were slightly clipped, like he was fighting to stay on his feet or fighting something else, although she couldn't imagine what.

She couldn't help it, her fingers brushed his skin, and in order to try not to focus on what that did to her, she said, "I can't believe all the colors in the bruise on your side here. That's the worst bruise I've ever seen. And I've seen some doozies."

"I'm sure you have, working at the sale barn." He grunted. "What happened to me surely isn't the first time that's happened."

"No. Not even close, but usually I don't have to take care of the aftereffects too much." She tugged the wrap a little tighter as she reached around front, switching from her left hand to her right again. "We've all had scrapes and bruises, but normally we take care of them ourselves. And nothing this bad," she added hastily, so he didn't think that she was saying that they had all been able to take care of themselves while he couldn't. She wasn't insinuating that at all.

He didn't say anything, so she continued, "I know this would have been me if you hadn't stepped in."

"Thought we said we weren't talking about that anymore," he said, kind of gruffly.

"I didn't want you to think that there was something wrong with you needing someone to help. Because there isn't."

"I know. I guess it's just a man thing."

"I figured. Although I would have trouble asking for help as well. Just... Just something about not being seen as capable, or I don't know. Just not wanting to not be able to take care of yourself."

"Yeah."

The wrap ended in the back again, with Velcro that would keep it up. She patted it down and then stepped around in front of him, leaving plenty of space between them.

He smelled too good, his presence felt right, and his need for help, far from making her not respect him or think he was incompetent, made her want to do as much as she could to help him. Whatever it took.

"How does that feel?" She forced her lips into some semblance of a smile and tried to pretend her breathing was just as normal as it ever was. "Is it tight enough?"

Part of her hoped that he'd say it wasn't, and she had to do it again, and part of her hoped he would say yes and walk away so she could run to her room and slam the door behind her, and work on pulling herself back together in the privacy of her bedroom.

She couldn't imagine having this reaction to anyone else. And was kind of surprised that she had with Armstrong.

She patched her brother up more than once and never had a problem with it, so she knew it wasn't the bruises or the idea of an injury.

It was Armstrong himself. Odd.

"It's fine. I appreciate you doing it. It... It feels good to be clean."

"You look like you're getting some of your color back too, so I think maybe you're going to be okay. I was a little worried since things got a little hairy down there in the kitchen."

"I couldn't tell. You looked pretty cool. Which made me think that maybe it wasn't as bad as what it felt."

"I was getting ready to pick you up off the floor. Thinking I wasn't sure whether I should call an ambulance or not."

"Thanks. I'll keep that in mind. Your facial expression doesn't give your thoughts away."

"I'm usually not very good at hiding them, but I didn't want you to get scared, and I didn't want you to think I was hovering or worrying."

"You haven't hovered or made me think you were worried. Actually, I was on the verge of thinking you didn't care."

She tilted her head at him and noted the slight tilt of one side of his mouth. "You're kidding. You're making a joke. I can't believe it. I didn't know you joked."

"It's a special occasion. First shower in three days calls for a little celebration joke."

"Oh. So it doesn't happen all the time. Just on special occasions like showers and stuff."

"This might surprise you, but when my ribs aren't broken, I shower regularly."

"I guess I'll have to believe that when I see it," she said, rather airily.

He grunted, and it was a laugh too. "I guess if you're here all summer, eventually I'm gonna stop hurting, and you'll see. At least once a week, and sometimes twice if I really feel I need it."

"That's great. I think I'll take over teaching the children about hygiene, and you can take over the farm work when you're ready."

He snorted again. "Quit making me laugh. It hurts every time."

"Sorry, but you started it."

He rolled his eyes. "Sometimes you're really mature, but just then, you sounded like a five-year-old."

"I know. I have sisters, and sometimes I can't stand all the maturity in the house and have to be a goofball."

"Really?" His tone said he didn't quite believe that and thought maybe she was kidding.

"Actually, I'm not really the jokester in the family. But it is fun to laugh. Although I'll try to respect the fact that it hurts you. Actually, I suppose I ought to go to my room, I need to take a shower of my own." She laughed, grateful it didn't hurt her ribs to do so.

"Eh, once every three days or so is plenty. After all, that's all I did, and I still had a woman crawling all over me today."

"If you're gonna stand there and joke, I don't want you complaining if I make you laugh again and your ribs hurt."

She was strangely reluctant to start toward her room, but even though he was smiling and seemed kind of relaxed and in no hurry to get to his own room, the whiteness around his mouth and the tightness beside his eyes showed clearly that he was still in pain, and he probably needed to sit down.

"I'll see you in the morning," she said, pulling herself away and walking to her room, even though she didn't want to.

He didn't move until her hand was on the knob. She pulled her door open, stepping through, closing it, and leaning against it, wondering what in the world she'd gotten herself into.

Chapter 9

My husband has this amazing talent - he makes me fall in love
with him every day. That's what makes our marriage last.
Plus he makes me laugh. We're living happily ever laughter.
- Janet Jolley from Providence, Utah

Maybe this wasn't such a good idea.

Armstrong winced as Daniel pulled on his hand. He'd been feeling pretty good all day.

Maybe getting a shower last night hadn't done anything for his actual physical healing, but it had been good for his mental health.

Having a fresh wrap on had provided stability for his ribs as well, and he could tell a huge difference today.

But probably having Glory help him had been the biggest thing.

He didn't really want to admit it, but that was why he was here at the auction tonight.

Because the idea of spending the evening at home, alone without her, had been depressing.

Adam stopped at the second row down and turned back to him, questions in his eyes. He nodded at his oldest son, and Adam filed into the row.

The seats were just basically big, long boxes on the floor, with no backs or sides.

The place buzzed with excitement, the auctioneer was down in the box in his place, and beyond the low-hanging ceiling, he could see animals being moved in the back.

He couldn't pick Glory out, but he didn't spend a lot of time trying, either. He needed to watch where he was going, focus on not moving the wrong way.

He'd taken a pain pill before he left, and while they made him sleepy, they always took the edge off the pain.

Of course, he hadn't considered that he'd be sitting on what basically amounted to a hard board.

It wasn't like he hadn't seen Glory all day, but it had been hard to watch her leave after the boys had been put down for their naps.

Which was crazy, since she'd only been at his house a few days.

Especially after last night. He wasn't sure exactly what had been going on, for him, whether it was a combination of gratitude toward his caregiver and gratitude toward the person who was taking care of his children, or whether it was true attraction.

Whatever it was, he couldn't remember ever feeling like that before. Hot and cold, like he wanted to run away and get closer, like he wanted to talk to her forever and find out everything he could about her, her hopes and dreams, her plans for the future, her favorite things.

He'd never been that interested in someone before and could barely keep his mouth shut around the questions that wanted to tumble out when he was around her.

It wasn't any easier than fisting his hands so he didn't grab a hold of her shoulders and pull her toward him.

Today she acted like nothing happened, and he figured all the confusion was on his end.

Still, even though he'd come to that conclusion, here he was, at the auction with four little boys, not planning on buying anything, just here because he wanted to be able to catch a glimpse of Glory, even knowing she would be home tonight, and he would see her tomorrow.

It was the kind of thing a lovesick teenager would do.

Not an adult father of four.

He settled down, prepared to help as Daniel climbed up on the seat beside him but allowing his son to do it by himself.

After giving Adam and Benjamin money to go get cheese fries to share with their brothers, he turned his eyes toward the arena where Coleman was already in position, and a calf was already on the scale waiting to be let out into the arena and become the first animal sold this evening.

A flash of blond caught his eye behind the scale, and he saw Glory, cattle prod in her hand, following a lumbering old Holstein down the aisle.

He didn't mean to stare, but his eyes caught and held; she just wore a sweatshirt, despite the North Dakota chill, and a pair of jeans and muck boots.

Her eyes were on the animal she followed, and her hair was pulled back in a ponytail, giving her a young, youthful look.

He couldn't miss the red cheeks, the half grin. She was always smiling. Always happy. Always with a can-do attitude. How could he not be attracted to that?

"Daddy, can I have some fries, too?" Caleb asked beside him as Benjamin and Adam came back, each holding a boat of long, golden fries slathered in steaming, yellow cheese.

He started to look toward his son, when Glory's head turned, almost as though she could feel his eyes on her. Their gazes met.

He'd been caught staring, and his cheeks heated, although she probably couldn't tell since he had several days' worth of beard growth on his face.

She had no way of knowing how long he'd been watching her, but it was still embarrassing.

Just the fact that he was here, and now she knew it. She knew how sore he'd been, how laid up, how much pain, and yet, he was here.

Her eyes widened, and her mouth opened, her step kind of stumbling, still she looked at him for another second or two before she tore her gaze away and walked out of sight. Following the cow.

"Daddy? I'm hungry," Caleb said, even though they'd eaten before they came.

"They're going to share, just give them a minute to sit down," he said as the gate opened, and the calf on the scale stepped out.

The auctioneer began speaking.

The auction had begun.

His ribs already hurt, and he was one hundred percent sure he should have stayed home, lying down on the couch.

The hard bench wasn't helping him at all.

They had run five calves through, and his boys were eating their fries, and he was tying Caleb's shoe, trying to pretend it didn't hurt his ribs to lean forward, when a shadow fell over him, and he looked up.

"I wasn't expecting to see you here tonight," Glory said, brows raised but a smile on her face.

"Miss Glory!" Benjamin and Caleb said together, while Adam, almost always serious, actually smiled.

Daniel wiggled off the seat and held his hands up for her to pick him up.

She leaned over the seat in front of her, reaching forward to grab him. When she had him settled on her hip, she looked at Armstrong, who had finished tying Caleb's shoe and straightened, trying even harder not to grimace.

"Just seemed like a good thing to do on a cold spring evening," he said, knowing he sounded stupid.

"That hard bench has to be hurting you," she said, concern in her voice, but as usual, she wasn't hovering. He didn't feel smothered.

"It is." He figured he could admit how stupid he was or just keep his mouth shut. He chose the second.

He hadn't noticed that the auction had paused, but suddenly Coleman appeared beside Glory.

"Why don't you take him up to the loft?" His hand landed on her shoulder, his mouth next to her ear. "The camp chairs there would be a lot comfier than these seats."

Chapter 10

Saying I'm sorry, and meaning it, often.
- Lynn from Sparks, NV

G lory jerked her head at her brother, then she looked down to the arena where the auction had paused while Coleman came up to talk to them. It wasn't completely uncommon for Coleman, or even the auctioneer, to see something that needed taking care of, and everyone just waited while they did it.

They didn't stand on ceremony here.

"That's a good idea," she said. She hadn't thought about the loft, but it was perfect for Armstrong and his kids while he wasn't feeling the best.

"I'll tell everyone they'll have to cover for you. You stay with him." Coleman jerked his chin at Armstrong, although Glory opened her mouth to argue. She never left her post. Never didn't do her job.

But something in Coleman's eyes made her pause, and then Daniel reached out and touched the gold chain that was just visible at the back of Coleman's neck, sticking out from under his shirt.

Glory knew Coleman had a ring attached to it. As far as she knew, he never took it off.

A woman's ring, from the diamond on it, but she didn't know what woman or what the significance of the ring was. Coleman had never said, and after one of her sisters had asked and been rudely shut down, none of them had tried again.

Coleman didn't say anything to Daniel, other than smiling at him and tweaking his nose which made Daniel laugh.

Then his gaze went to Adam. "Would you like to come down to the arena with me?"

Adam's eyes grew big, and he lifted them to his dad for permission.

Glory almost laughed when Armstrong didn't look concerned, didn't ask Coleman for assurances that he'd watch him or assurances that he would stay safe.

All he said was, "You can go. But you better listen."

Adam nodded eagerly, and then his eyes went to Coleman with almost hero worship in them.

"You can help me with these calves. Sometimes they get a little stubborn."

Glory smiled as Adam eagerly followed Coleman down the steps, ducking under the fence and through the little gate that was well camouflaged but always there, leading from the arena seats to the arena itself.

If Armstrong were a woman, she would have assured him that Adam wouldn't be hurt dealing with the little calves. And Coleman would watch him carefully.

Coleman seemed pretty tough, but with five sisters, he definitely had a soft side, although like most men, he hid it.

"Can you climb the stairs?" she asked Armstrong, knowing he had at home, but the stairs here were steeper.

"I can. Probably can't do it while I'm carrying Daniel," he said, his tone low, like he didn't want anyone around them hearing him admit to his weakness.

She understood that. "I've got him." She held a hand out for Caleb, who took it without question.

The time she'd spent with them this week had allowed them to warm up to her, and while they weren't perfect and didn't listen perfectly, she felt like she had a good relationship with them. They weren't afraid of her, and they liked her.

"So where is the loft?" Armstrong asked, once they'd gotten up out of the arena seating area and walked around the back.

She looked up, above the payment room in the back, and nodded her head.

His head went up, and his eyes widened when he saw the open area above the payment room, guarded by bars, almost like a jail cell.

"My sisters and Coleman and I always used to love to play there when we were little. We kind of imagined that it was a special place for buyers who maybe didn't want to be seen by the rest of the crowd to stay, when they first built the barn. But we really don't know. It didn't come with records."

She walked out the door that led to the stairs to go down to the pen area. Instead of turning left though, she twisted a nail and opened the door that was always there but blended into the woodwork so well most people didn't know about it.

"That's slick," he said.

"Yeah. It fits so tightly, people don't know it's there. We hardly ever use it during an auction, and it's just kind of our little secret. Although it's not really a secret."

They went through. It got even darker when Glory shut the door behind them, but once they stepped up, the light from the barred opening shone on the floor, lighting it and showing that there wasn't anything there aside from a couple of chairs.

Benjamin, who still had what was left of his fries in one hand, said, "Wow! This is cool. Too bad Adam isn't here."

"You can tell him all about it later," Glory said, smiling at his stunned expression.

As she was walking up the stairs, Daniel had gripped her neck tight, as it was pretty dark, but once they came up out of the dark stairwell, his arms loosened, and his little head craned all around.

"The bars are close enough together that we shouldn't have to worry about the boys falling through them. The only thing we have to watch is right here," Glory said, indicating where the floor stopped right at the stairwell.

"Boys. You need to stay away from that," Armstrong said immediately, pointing to the edge. "Looks like you can play pretty much anywhere here, but you want to be careful not to fall off of that ledge."

"Orchid actually did fall off once. She screamed bloody murder and cut her arm, but nothing was broken, almost miraculously, I think, looking back."

"Good to know a fall is survivable, but in the meantime, let's hope they don't fall."

She agreed, and from what she'd observed of his children in the past few days, they really listened to him. He had trained them well; she didn't have any complaints about it.

"Right there are the camp chairs that Coleman was talking about. I think that'll be easier on your ribs than the hard boards down below. Although, it might be kind of hard to get out of."

She could never quite tell what would hurt him and what wouldn't. And maybe it just depended on how his pain pills were working.

He nodded. "If you don't mind, I'll take the bigger one. I think it'll be easy to sit in but hard to get out of."

"That's fine. I think I'll sit on the floor. Maybe Daniel wants to sit on my lap."

The auctioneer's voice came up to them, raising and lowering as he took bids and did his singsong chant.

"You don't have to sit on the floor," Armstrong said, sounding put out. Like he was annoyed that he was taking a chair, and she had to sit on the floor.

"There's a second chair, but one of the kids can have it. I kinda like sitting on the floor right next to the bars, and it's been forever since I've done that and watched the auction. Usually I have to work."

"So you're saying you want me to break my ribs more often to get you out of having to work at the auction so you can just sit here and watch it?"

It was the light teasing that he'd done last night. It immediately transported her back to them standing in the hall, his chest bare except the wrap, and her feeling all the things she shouldn't be feeling for the man she was helping.

She looked at Daniel and rubbed her nose to his before she pointed out his brother. "Look. There's Adam."

He turned his head, searching in the direction that she pointed, before he squealed Adam's name and clapped.

"Maybe you could just pretend to break ribs, because I don't think I would ever ask anyone to go through the kind of pain you've been going through for me."

"Not even to get out of work?"

"I love my work. I love what I do. I love getting to work with my family. I love being involved in agriculture and getting to help the farmers in the area. They all come at some point, and you just feel like you're right in the middle of everything. Can't imagine doing anything else."

"Taking care of a man and his four kids?"

He hadn't been looking at her, but his mouth snapped shut. He looked straight out through the bars almost directly facing the auctioneer. It was like he realized how what he said sounded. That's what a wife did. Took care of a man and his children.

She almost teased him about it. Like, he wanted to marry her.

Maybe, if they hadn't had whatever happened last night, where her feelings really did go over the line, she would have. She probably could have gotten him to smile about it. But after last night, she wasn't sure what exactly they were.

Or maybe she just wasn't sure how he felt. Up until that point, she hadn't really thought about it and hadn't cared, but all of a sudden, last night changed things, and now she found she did.

She sat on her butt, her legs folded and crossed in front of her, and Daniel plopped down in the middle of her lap, with Caleb coming over and scrunching down beside her on his knees, his hands on his legs and his body leaning forward like he wanted to get just a little closer so he could see better.

She smiled at his position and even at Benjamin, who didn't sit down but stood by the bars, one hand on a bar, one hand shoved in his pocket as he watched his brother.

"Maybe Coleman will let you help with them next time," she said to Benjamin. His head jerked toward her, and his eyes widened while his brows lifted.

"Do you think he would?"

She nodded. "I'm pretty sure he would. Looks like Adam is doing a good job, and I can tell him I think you'd do almost as well, even if you're a little bit smaller."

"When I'm as big as Adam, I'll be able to work just as hard as he can."

"I'm sure you will. You're both hard workers, and I've appreciated your help the past few days. I know your dad has too, and he's really needed it since he hasn't felt very well."

"When I get big, Daddy can be hurt all the time, and I'll do everything."

Glory tried to keep her lips from smiling at the idea that Armstrong would be hurt all the time. She was pretty sure he wasn't going to go along with that plan, but they had some years to discuss things and perhaps come to an agreement that both of them could get on board with.

"I'm sure you'll be a great help when you get bigger, especially since you're such a good help now." He smiled at her before he turned back to the auction, watching intently.

He was the kind of kid who would pay attention to the details, and when it was his turn, he would know exactly what Adam had done and be able to do it himself. As much as he was able.

Adam was a lot more confident, bold, and outgoing. While Benjamin was more of a thinker.

It's funny how children were often so different in personality, even though they had the same parents. She could pick out little bits and pieces of Armstrong in each one of his boys. Pieces of his personality, different ways they looked like him.

Daniel cuddled in her lap, pointing at something and babbling about it, and she pulled her mind back to the present. Loving the way the loft felt cozy and private, but at the same time, they could see everything that was going on, with a bird's-eye view.

She could see why it had been built and when people might have used it.

However, Armstrong shifted beside her, making her feel that he wasn't completely comfortable but was as relaxed as he'd been so far with the pain of the broken ribs, so she settled into watching, just enjoying the fun feeling of being together, almost like a family. And funny, but as she watched, seeing Adam do such a great job helping Coleman with the calves, she couldn't have been more proud of him if she'd been his real mother.

That scared her a little, and she felt like she needed to be careful. She was only taking care of these children. She was only helping this man. She wasn't becoming part of their family. She needed to be careful to remember that and to remind her heart.

She didn't want it to get broken.

Chapter 11

CCD! Choice, we need to choose to love and support each other. Commitment, we choose to be committed to each other, and Decision, we decide to support our marriage. In my case, I decided early that divorce was not going to be a top of the list answer or threat. Fortunately, we have not needed to deal with any form of abuse or damaging addictions. We also have benefited from shared faith.
- Madelyn Neher from Minnesota

The next morning, Armstrong woke to the smell of bacon.

He lay in bed for about three seconds, his eyes closed, just breathing deeply, before his eyes flew open and he jerked the covers off, jarring his ribs. Pain shot up his side and down his leg and made his breath catch in his lungs.

That had been stupid, but he couldn't believe he was lying in bed while Glory was up cooking.

The very least he could do would be to get the stock fed and the chores done before church so she didn't have to do everything.

He could even hear his boys, some of them at least, their chatter drifting up the stairs, along with Glory's muted laugh.

She was deliberately trying to be quiet so he could sleep.

He felt lazy. What kind of man was he that he was allowing a woman, this woman who had worked at her family's auction the night before, get up before him and do his work? Take care of his children? And she probably was expecting to do the farm chores as well.

It had been a late night, and she'd been up even later than he was, helping to put the children to bed and getting food out for lunch today.

She had to be just as tired as he was, and yet he was lying around in bed like he didn't have a farm to run and a family to take care of.

Moving a little slower, conscious of the ribs that now ached, he got himself dressed and ready and went downstairs.

Bacon sizzled on the stove, and two of his boys stood at the counter on either side of Glory while she helped them crack eggs.

"Do I have time to do the chores before that's ready?" he asked, figuring he probably didn't but wanting to do something.

"Hey! Good morning," she said, turning and smiling, her hand on Daniel, unconsciously making sure he didn't fall off his chair.

He loved that her concern was for their safety and welfare, even when she was distracted with something else.

He waited, and she spoke again. "I already did the chores. I was up early," she said, grinning and shrugging at his expression. After all, how early had she gotten up in order to be done with the chores, have breakfast almost ready, and with all of that, she was smiling and in a good mood and having the patience to allow his two youngest sons to help her.

"I guess I can go and get the other two boys up then."

"They're actually in the bathtub right now. Although, if you want to let them know that breakfast is ready and they need to get out, you could do that." Her smile was bright and not at all offended that she'd been doing all the work herself.

In fact, nothing in her words or actions or even expressions indicated that she was the slightest bit upset with him.

Still, he felt like he needed to apologize.

"I'm sorry I slept in. I don't usually do that."

"I tried to be extra quiet. I know that it's hard for you to sit back and let someone else do things, and it's really good for you to get a little extra rest. Your body can heal faster." She was still smiling, but her words were serious. She really meant it.

Her concern was seriously for him to get better.

He wasn't paying her enough, not for this kind of attention or this kind of care and concern. Actually, he'd hired her for the children. Not even for him.

He'd always admired someone who would go above and beyond, considered himself that kind of person.

It wasn't too often that he got to work with someone like that.

"Actually, never mind. I hear the bathroom door opening, and it sounds like the boys are out."

It had been so late when they got home last night, they hadn't made anyone take baths, so they all needed them.

"I figured I'd put the two little boys in the tub after we eat. After all, we know they're going to get messy again." She lifted her brow and looked down at the little boys, who smiled right back at her.

"Then I guess the only thing left for me to do is set the table." He moved toward the cupboard, passing along behind her, smelling her clean, fresh, happy scent, which reminded him of sunshine and rainbows and a life with no worries.

It wasn't that she didn't have worries. She just...she just seemed to be able to smile through them anyway.

His mind immediately wanted to compare her to Blanche, but he tried not to.

Blanche was in his past; she'd left. Didn't want him anymore. Didn't want their kids.

Whether she was a grouch in the morning, whether she lay in bed and allowed him to do all the work, and whether she complained and was miserable, it didn't matter. He would have stayed with her no matter what.

But...

It was interesting to note that there were people who were happy in the morning. People who seemed to enjoy their work. Women who didn't see the children as a nuisance but saw them and treated them like precious souls who needed love and attention.

He got the plates in his hand and turned, when he realized that Caleb was standing beside him looking up, blinking.

"Can I help?" he asked, a little shyly.

He supposed he was guilty of the very things that he had been thinking about with Blanche. It was always faster to do the work without the kids helping.

Sure, they were around all the time, but they usually played beside him while he worked. He didn't always take the time to give them little jobs and to let them do them themselves while he supervised, not the way Glory was doing right now with Daniel and cracking eggs.

He'd already splattered one on the floor, and even now she was bending over cleaning it up.

"You sure can," he said, handing two plates to Caleb. "Be careful. They'll break if you drop them."

Caleb's head nodded up and down as he walked to the table, carrying the plates like they were the crown jewels of the Netherlands.

"We need a dog," he said, looking at Glory on her hands and knees scooping up the broken egg.

She grinned. "I have to agree with you. It would clean this up for me, and I wouldn't have had to worry about a thing."

"Although maybe there's enough chaos in the kitchen," he said, wondering if she was really as immune to it as she seemed.

"I grew up with four sisters. Of course there was Coleman, too, but he didn't really contribute to the chaos. But the five of us... It was nuts from the time we got up until we went to bed at night. And fun. I miss it sometimes. But the boys remind me of my siblings and I when we were little. Everyone should have a happy childhood like that."

He supposed he couldn't disagree. Funny how childhood represented such a small part of a person's life but such a huge part of their lifetime memories.

What a blessing to have a life where those memories that you never forgot were happy ones, full of fun and cheer and all the things that made a person feel warm and safe and loved.

He definitely wanted that for his boys, but he felt like he already failed them. After all, didn't a person need to have their mother stay with them in order to feel warm and happy and safe and loved?

He hadn't been able to keep his wife. Hadn't been able to keep her happy, hadn't been able to get her to stay.

Hadn't been enough for her.

"I need more, Daddy." Caleb looked up at him expectantly, the plates that he'd had set haphazardly on the table kind of in front of the chairs but a little lopsided.

"Here you go," he said as his two oldest boys came down the stairs. Adam's eyes were still shining, despite his tiredness, and if Armstrong had to guess, it was because of Coleman's allowing him to help with the calves.

After they'd gotten done with the calves, Glory had gone down and gotten him and brought him up to the loft, where he kind of floated on a little cloud, watching the rest of the auction with fascination.

"Do you think Mr. Coleman will be in church today?" Adam asked as they came to the table.

"Probably. He usually is," Armstrong said.

"Do you think he'll let me help him again?" Adam's brows were up and his look eager.

Armstrong hesitated. He wasn't sure why Coleman had allowed him to help. Whether it was because Glory was with them, whether he knew Armstrong was laid up. He couldn't make any promises to his son.

"I'm sure he will," Glory said. "I'm pretty sure he'll let Benjamin help as well. And you guys can help in the back with me, too. It's not quite as exciting as being in front of everyone, but we get to see all the different animals and move them around. I love it." It was easy to hear the passion in her voice and her true love for what she did.

That was something that maybe he'd lost a little of when his wife left him. He had been born to be a farmer, had wanted to farm all his life, but some of the joy of living had been taken away when Blanche had left him with everything, all the cares and worries and the pressure of taking care of all the children and being a mom and dad and still providing for them and paying the bills, and everything had just felt crushing.

Funny how having someone with him, someone to stand beside him, someone to encourage him and help him and complete him, made all the difference in the world. Maybe it was a mental thing.

But...maybe part of the reason that Blanche had left was because...he hadn't been what she needed.

His eyes went to Glory, still standing at the counter. She had a spatula in her hand and had just finished flipping the eggs over easy.

Maybe he shouldn't look for someone else, if he didn't know how to take care of his wife properly. After all, if he was getting everything he needed from her, but he wasn't giving her what she needed, what kind of husband was he?

And maybe that was getting the cart ahead of the horse, maybe he should be more concerned about whether or not he was being a friend and reciprocating the friendship he'd been offered.

Like the woman standing at the stove. Sure, he was paying her to be there. But he wasn't paying her to be what she was—kind and sweet and cheerful. Caring of his children, concerned about him, offering her family and their business and everything she had, just opening it up and giving him anything he needed.

That's what a friend did.

Had he done it for his friends? For her?

Not to anyone. And certainly not to Glory. He had never been anything to her. And yet... She hadn't hesitated to offer anything in her power to be what he needed her to be.

That was the kind of friend a person wanted to have.

That was the kind of friend he wanted to be. Even if nothing developed between Glory and him—he thought of the night she'd removed his bandage wrappings and figured maybe he wanted something to develop—but even if nothing did, he wanted to be her friend. And he wanted to be as good a friend to her as she had been to him.

It was going to require some growth on his part. Because he wasn't used to thinking about others the way she did. He was more used to thinking about himself. Just surviving.

Of course, he needed to put his family first, but he wanted to be more than just a self-centered taker who never looked around at others or reciprocated the kind things that people did to him.

He wanted to be more. Glory had inspired him. He should thank her.

Chapter 12

Communication!
- Priscilla - Perth from Western Australia

"Hey, Mom, what can I do to help?" Glory said as she walked into the kitchen. Her mom stood at the stove stirring something, while Orchid and Lavender set the table.

"Just sit down and take a break. From what I hear, you've been working pretty hard." Her mom glanced over her shoulder before turning back to the stove.

"We've all been hearing that. Someone said that Armstrong would be a handful, because he wouldn't take being laid up easy. I kind of pictured you having to pick him up off the floor all the time," Lavender said with a grin as she set a plate down, adjusting the silverware beside it.

"Well, that hasn't exactly happened. But he is kind of stubborn. A typical man."

"Maybe a typical man from the men that you grew up around, but not all men are hard workers, and not all men work through the pain. In fact, sometimes they turn into big babies when they hurt." Her mom didn't turn around as she spoke, but her words carried easily in her cultured, calm voice.

Glory supposed she was right. She only had grown up around North Dakota men. Country boys. Guys who knew how to work, how to fix things, how to get things done.

Although Rose's husband, Derek, had been in The Cities for a decade. Maybe he had changed some, but he still had that North Dakota toughness.

"I don't really want to know any other kind of man," she said a little carelessly. Because it was true. She'd seen a few TV shows where the men seemed a little wimpy, more concerned about what other people thought and what other people were doing than actually making a difference with their own life.

Funny, the men she was around didn't exactly go around thinking they wanted to make a difference with their lives. They just did it.

"It takes all kinds to make the world go around," her mom said, sounding wiser than Glory's thoughts for sure. "And I don't think you should look down on any kind of man. Because God made them all. But a lot of times, where we grow up affects our thinking and what we believe. You can't discount that."

Glory didn't say anything, because she figured it was probably true. Her mom had traveled a lot more than she had. She was a homebody and really didn't have any desire to go anywhere. But not traveling meant that a person didn't really see what was going on in the rest of the world.

"He seems like he'd be kind of grumpy. I don't know how you can stand to be around a grouch all day," Orchid said. She was more quiet than Lavender, but she wasn't without an opinion.

"He's not. He's actually kind of funny. And I've only known him when he's been in pain. So, the fact that he can joke even though he's hurting impresses me."

"I want a man that can make me laugh. I won't even look at him if he doesn't look like he's funny," Lavender said, opening up the refrigerator door and grabbing the pitcher of iced tea.

"He's definitely funny. But it's more of a muted humor. He's not constantly cracking jokes. Just has funny observations that aren't...put-downs, you know? Like he's not being derisive toward other people, which is a kind of humor I hate."

It was true. She didn't like that kind of sly humor where people made fun of other people and kind of laughed about it. Even if she didn't understand all the different kinds of men in the world, as her mom had implied, it didn't mean she wanted to laugh at them or act like she was somehow better than they were. Because that's kind of what it was, looking at other people and thinking they weren't as good, when a person had to make fun of them.

"I thought you guys looked like you were cozy there, both of you helping with the kids, and I did catch you guys laughing with each other," Marigold said as she stepped into the room.

Glory had heard the front door open but hadn't stopped setting napkins around the table to check to see who it was, figuring it was one of her other two sisters or possibly Coleman.

"Is Coleman coming today?" she asked her mom, ignoring Marigold.

Maybe she had been laughing with Armstrong. She'd definitely been helping with his kids, and the thought that they probably looked like an old married couple had crossed her mind as well. Except she didn't ever want to be an old married couple. She always wanted to have fun and enjoy her husband. After all, if she was going to get married to someone and stay with him for the rest of her life, she wanted him to be her best friend, someone she could laugh with and enjoy life with for decades.

She didn't want him to be someone that she ended up not being able to stand and always trying to get away from. The way a lot of married couples seemed.

"I'm here. What do you want?" Coleman drawled, coming around and putting his arm around her shoulders.

"I wanted to thank you for letting Adam help you yesterday. He just floated around the rest of the evening, and first thing he said when he came downstairs this morning was 'do you think he'll let me help again?'"

Coleman smiled. Not huge, but a pleased grin. "He did a good job. You can tell him I said so."

"I'll tell him, but if you see him again, you should tell him. He... I'm pretty sure he idolizes you at this point."

Coleman jerked his head and didn't say anything, but Glory figured it probably made him a little nervous to think that other little boys were looking up at him, using him as a role model.

It was true though. All the little boys at the sale looked at him and wanted to be just like him someday.

They'd grow out of it eventually, of course, most of them anyway. Latching on to bigger dreams. Dreams that would take them away from their home probably, but still, the idea that he was down there in front of everyone was always something that Coleman remembered.

At least, from the few times that he talked about it, Glory knew he felt a heavy responsibility to be a good role model.

"So, Glory, you ignored me," Marigold said, her face coming over Glory's other shoulder, opposite from Coleman. "You two looked like a cute married couple." She repeated her statement, apparently in case Glory had forgotten what she'd said.

"Well, I'm helping him with his children, and he hired me because he doesn't have a wife. I suppose it makes a little bit of sense that we might look like that."

"It's one thing to help someone with their children, it's another thing to laugh and look so comfortable with them you might have been with them for ten years," Marigold said, her hand resting lightly on her baby bump.

"The way you and I do," Dodge, her husband, said as he leaned his head over Marigold's shoulder the way Marigold had hers over Glory's.

"The only difference being you and I really have known each other that long, while as far as I know, Glory just met Armstrong."

"We've known him for years," Glory said, hating that her voice sounded defensive. And knowing, even as she said it, that she was being ridiculous. They'd known of him, but it wasn't like she and Armstrong had been friends for years.

They did seem to be able to get along okay. In fact, she felt comfortable with him in a way she didn't usually feel. But at the same time, there was this attraction that probably accounted for the defensiveness of her voice. She didn't want her family thinking, knowing, that she was attracted to the man she was working for. That would make them protective, for one thing, and for another, she would feel like she had to prove that she wasn't doing anything wrong.

Which she wasn't.

But since she was living at his house, it was especially important that everything was aboveboard. For her anyway. Just because she didn't want to give anyone the idea that she was doing something that was morally wrong.

Just like there were little boys watching Coleman, she knew there were girls watching her. Watching to see what kind of person she was, what kind of values and morals she lived, especially since she was active in the church, and they expected her to live what she taught.

She wanted to. She didn't want to be the kind of person who went to church, taught the Bible, and then didn't live it.

Not to mention, she didn't want God to have to forgive her over and over and over again for the same sins.

She didn't like to do that with other people. Forgiving once was one thing, but forgiving again and again? For the same thing? She wanted them to learn their lesson, to be punished for what they'd done wrong, not to just be cleanly forgiven.

Even though that's what God commanded.

She didn't want God to have to do that to her. Forgive her free and clean every time, without her doing anything to try to fix it or change it or stop transgressing his law.

"I thought they looked cute together. Sometimes people do," their mother said, and Coleman and Marigold turned. Dodge kept his arm around Marigold, keeping her close to him.

Glory's eyes hooked on them for just a moment. They looked so happy together. Marigold practically glowed, and Dodge obviously didn't want her to leave his side. He was protective, and he adored her.

Marigold knew how blessed she was to have someone like Dodge, and he obviously knew the same.

Was that the key to a successful relationship? That each person in it felt like they'd been given a gift of immeasurable value?

Glory wasn't sure. She wasn't sure what to look for in a mate. Just knew she didn't want to have a marriage that didn't work. Didn't want to have to go through the pain of divorce. Because she was the kind of person who, when she did something, put everything, her heart and soul and all she was, into it.

Marriage would be the same for her. She didn't want to put everything she had into a marriage only to have it break up, because...she felt like she'd be shattered beyond repair.

Maybe she'd been playing it safe and hadn't even been realizing it. Staying away from relationships, because she knew if one didn't work out, she'd never recover from the pain of a breakup. Most definitely would never recover from the pain of a divorce.

"Isn't that what you've always said marriage should be, Mom?" Lavender said as she finished pouring the last glass of tea. "Two people who work well together?"

"That's one way. I think that there are different kinds of good marriages though. Sometimes, people are just compatible. Sometimes, they're exactly the same, and they can finish each other's sentences. But other times, they're completely opposite, and the things that one of them does well, the other one doesn't, and their strengths cover the other's weakness. I don't know that there's any one criterion that makes a good marriage."

Her mother didn't often talk about that type of thing. She'd been devastated when their father had died and had thrown herself into raising her big family and keeping the business going. There'd been one, rather notorious, time she dated Mr. Powers. But it had ended in a disaster, and the Piece Makers quilting group had been blamed.

Regardless, Glory hung on her every word, because as she recalled, her parents had had an amazing marriage, with her dad being happy and her mom glowing every day.

That was the kind of marriage she wanted.

You can't have a marriage like that if you're not willing to take the risk of the pain it could involve.

She closed her eyes and tried to shove the voice away. Even though she knew it was right. She always had very good surface relationships but never wanted to dig deep with anyone, because... Maybe she was afraid of being disappointed too. But definitely the pain. She couldn't take it. She knew that.

"Are you going back tonight?" Lavender asked as they all settled in their chairs.

"Yeah. He told me to come home, take a break, take a nap, and he'd take care of feeding the kids, feeding the animals, and taking care of them today, and I told him I'd be back this evening to help him put them to bed."

"I'm glad you're there. The man needs someone. I can't imagine trying to do everything he's trying to do with broken ribs. That's one of the most painful things a man can work with." Coleman's voice was very matter-of-fact, no thoughts of romance or relationships in it. Even his face was serious.

They all bowed their heads, Coleman said grace, and Glory listened, but she also added a little prayer of her own, one asking the Lord to help her be brave. To help her not be afraid of the pain, if He was going to put a relationship in front of her, that she wouldn't miss it because she allowed her fear to direct her decisions.

Chapter 13

Nurturing your relationship every day.
- Kathy Winchell from Dalhart, Texas

"I wish your mom and I could come, son, but we already have your older sister's kids, and it's everything we can do to keep up with them. There's no way we can come down."

Armstrong stood on the front porch of his house, his two youngest children sleeping, the other two at school.

Glory had gone for groceries, and he'd given his dad a call.

Not really because he wanted anything, but because he hadn't heard from them for a while. Not since he texted and said he'd broken his ribs.

He hadn't expected anything at the time of the text. It just seemed like something his parents would want to know. He tried to be considerate, treating them the way he'd want his own children to treat him.

His mom had texted back saying to let her know if he needed anything.

He hadn't said anything else. Because, obviously, with broken ribs and four children, he needed a lot. But he didn't want to have to ask. And then Glory had stepped in, and he hadn't needed to.

Thankfully, since it sounded like his dad was busy.

Although he'd grown up outside of Bismarck, where his parents still lived, it had been his dream to own his own farm.

His mom was a nurse, and his dad a business exec.

They didn't know anything about farming and had no idea of the amount of work he was facing.

"Don't worry about it, Dad. I'm doing fine. I have someone helping me, and..." There was a pickup coming down the driveway, and he squinted.

It looked like Coleman's.

Just then, his phone buzzed with a text. He pulled it away from his ear to see what it said.

It was from Glory.

Coleman's coming. I met him in town and told him that the seed had arrived for you to overseed your pasture, but you weren't entirely sure that you'd be able to sit in a tractor seat for that long. He's coming out to do it. I told him where. He shouldn't need to bother you.

It was a long text, and by the end of it, he didn't know whether to be irritated that Glory was going around town telling everyone his business, or whether he should throw her a party when she came home in appreciation for everything she had done for him.

Again, that irritating feeling, the one that said that he wasn't giving nearly as much as she was in their relationship, whatever it was, nagged at him.

He didn't want to be the one who only took and didn't give.

He typed out, "thanks," and sent it, putting the phone back to his ear.

"Your sister's coming back from her cruise three days from now, if you still need help, I'm sure one of us can come over," his dad offered.

"I don't think you need to. People are taking care of me, and my ribs are feeling a lot better." It was true. They still hurt him every time he moved pretty much, but not the almost unbearable pain of freshly broken ribs. More like an ache, one that he could handle. It wasn't comfortable, but it was bearable.

"Well, that's good. I guess if you're going to break ribs, you need to do it when your sister isn't going on a cruise next time," his dad said, and Armstrong knew it was a joke.

He grunted, even though he wasn't entirely sure he found it funny.

But he didn't have any answers, not about what his parents should have done or his sister. The cruise had been spur-of-the-moment with her new boyfriend, and Armstrong supposed that having time away from her children was probably a priority in a new relationship.

As he thought that, he thought about Glory and wondered if maybe he should try to do something with her, without the children.

If she's what he was interested in.

He was interested. He just didn't know whether she was and didn't know whether it was a wise thing anyway. After all, she was helping him, he was paying her, so that made him her boss.

Were there laws against that?

Maybe that was just in the workplace. He wasn't sure. It didn't matter though, because it wasn't a good idea.

Coleman's pickup had gone straight to the barn, and Coleman got out, lifting a hand in acknowledgment of Armstrong standing on the porch before going around to the side of the barn where the tractor was.

He strode with confidence, so Armstrong figured that Glory had explained to him where the seed was, the planter, and the tractor as well. It was full of fuel since Armstrong had filled it up at the pump before he parked it, so Coleman shouldn't need anything.

"I just wanted to check and make sure you're okay. Glad to hear things are going well. I guess give me a call if you need anything," Armstrong said, as his dad remained silent, noise in the background of fighting and yelling, and his mom's voice over everything, telling everyone to calm down.

His sister just had three children. Two girls and a boy. Made Armstrong glad he had boys rather than girls, since they seemed to be louder and fight more.

"Sounds good. Come see us sometime," his dad said before he said goodbye and hung up.

Armstrong almost laughed. He probably wasn't going to have time to see his parents, but there was no point in telling his dad that.

Shoving his phone in his pocket, he stepped carefully off the porch, remembering in time that he couldn't stride like he normally did. Well, he could, but it would hurt a lot worse than gingerly setting his feet down as he walked.

Regardless, he went across the yard and around the side where the planter was, pulling the pin out of the hitch and making sure the PTO shaft was set to the side, figuring that Coleman would be around with the tractor, and he'd give him a hand hooking it up.

Just bending over squeezed his ribs and made the pain surge, but he tried to ignore it. After all, after he was done helping hook the planter up, he didn't have anything else to do all day. Other than to be grateful to his friends and neighbors who were taking care of him.

Sure enough, less than five minutes later, Coleman came around the side of the barn driving the tractor he had told Glory yesterday he would be using with the planter, when his ribs felt well enough.

Coleman grinned a little when he saw Armstrong standing there, then pulled ahead, turning and backing up, the hitch lined up perfectly.

Obviously, he'd done it a time or two before.

Armstrong dropped the pin in and was working on getting the PTO hooked together when Coleman came around the side of the tractor.

"Figured you wouldn't mind. Glory said she was texting you."

"She did. I appreciate it," Armstrong said, straightening and trying not to wince, although his lips felt tight. The pain was always worse when he bent over.

"I had a free afternoon and figured I'd enjoy it just as much sitting in a tractor, looking at the beautiful North Dakota sky, as I would sitting at home wondering what I should be doing."

Armstrong highly doubted that Coleman would be sitting around his house wondering what he could do, but he didn't say anything.

"I appreciate it. Ribs feel a lot better than they did last week, that's for sure, but it's going to be another week before I'm ready to bounce around at all."

"Figured. Don't worry about it if you're not feeling up to it, but if you bring the kids to the auction on Wednesday, your boy can give me a hand down in the arena when it starts."

"I appreciate that. He was really hoping you'd ask him."

"When I see him, I will. Now that I know it's okay." He let out a breath. "Glory said she'd take the other one back with her and have him work on moving some animals. We'll take care of him. Won't let him be around anything that might hurt him."

"I appreciate it. Accidents are part of life, but they aren't necessary if you're being careful."

"I believe that too," Coleman said, slapping him on the shoulder, doing it lightly, almost as though he wasn't sure how bad the ribs were hurting and didn't want to make them feel worse than what they did.

They grinned at each other, then Coleman walked back to the front of the tractor, and Armstrong stood back while he pulled away, taking the planter to the barn floor where the seed was stored.

Armstrong supposed he could open the bags, so he went up and gave as much help as he could, aware that sometimes when someone who really couldn't do a job was trying to help with the job anyway, they got in the way more than anything, so he made sure that that wasn't the case with him.

By the time he was done, he kind of wished he wouldn't have, because his ribs were aching, and it was another two hours before he could take a pain pill. He'd been trying to stretch his pain pills out longer, not liking the idea that he was on a strict schedule with them, depending on them to be able to function.

It was all he could do to walk across the yard and take his boots off before he collapsed, as gently as he could, onto the couch.

He'd worn himself out to the point where he didn't even hear Glory when she came home.

Chapter 14

Thinking of the needs of my spouse is a priority. When not
thinking of myself life is sweeter.
- Lissa Paxton from Meyersdale PA

"You don't have to go. I can handle the children." Glory's brows lifted as Armstrong descended the stairs Sunday morning, button up shirt and new jeans, his hair slicked back and his face freshly shaved.

"No. You have done enough. I couldn't possibly ask you to take my kids to church and to the hog roast afterwards by yourself. I know they've been looking forward to going, so I'm just going to hang in there." His eyes met hers. "Although, I don't think I'd be able to if you weren't going too. I appreciate it."

"I'm looking forward to it!" She grinned. She truly was. "Adam agreed to be my partner in the church race, and Benjamin and I are going to do the steer wrestling together."

"Wow. I didn't realize you had everything planned out."

"It only comes once a year. We're excited about it."

The kids gathered around and started chattering about the things they were looking forward to doing, and Armstrong listened with patience. He never seemed overwhelmed by all the chatter, even though he was a fairly calm, straightforward kind of guy. The kind of guy who didn't have a lot of noise or excitement going on around him all the time.

She bet his ex had probably told him he was boring.

But she didn't think so.

There was a lot to appreciate in a man like Armstrong. Someone who was solid and dependable.

"Maybe we should drive separately in case you get tired, or your ribs start to hurt to the point where you can't stand it, so you can come home." She had to suggest that, just because she didn't want him there, gritting his teeth through his pain and staying just because she and the kids were having a good time.

And she expected to have a good time.

Something passed over his face. She wasn't sure exactly what it was, but he didn't seem pleased with her idea.

He finished walking down the stairs before he answered her.

"I don't think I'm going to want to come home before it's over, but if you're afraid it's going to happen, I'm fine if we drive separately."

"I want to drive with Miss Glory!" Caleb shouted, wrapping an arm around Glory's hips.

Glory put an arm around his little shoulders and squeezed him into her. She felt like she'd gotten to know Caleb and Daniel really well with all the time they'd spent together at home.

The older two boys had been in school a good bit, and she didn't know them quite as well, but she made a point in the evenings for them to always do something fun together, even if they had a lot of schoolwork or housework to do.

As an adult, she didn't want to spend all of her days in drudgery, and she couldn't imagine that the children wanted that either.

Not to mention, her heart went out to them to have a broken home so early in their lives. Had to do something to them to think that their mom didn't want them.

Or, if they hadn't thought along those lines, at least wonder why she wasn't there.

Regardless, she thought of it as her duty to make sure that they had a good time in the evening.

Armstrong had gone along with her plan, although they'd never discussed it. Often he'd play with them, as much as his ribs would allow.

"You seem like you're feeling a lot better," she said, giving him a thorough look. His eyes weren't nearly as pinched as they had been, and while he wasn't moving with complete confidence, he didn't walk hunched over, with his arm across his stomach and acting like every move hurt.

"I almost have times where there is no pain. Not when I'm moving, but when I'm still, I can almost forget that they're broken."

"That's great. Sounds like you're healing."

"Can't be fast enough. Kills me to not be able to be out in the fields and to have to rely on other people to do it. Especially when I know those people are busy with their own things and really don't have time."

"You're giving people a chance to do something that makes them feel good. Because it always makes people feel good to do nice things for other people."

His lips flattened, but his eyes were thoughtful as he stared at her, like he hadn't considered that.

"Caleb, can you carry this out for me?" she asked, handing Caleb the container with fruit salad in it. The lid was on tight, and it wouldn't matter whether he dropped it on the ground, or hung it upside down.

"I get to help!" Caleb said, jumping over to the counter, like getting to help was the best thing in the world, but holding his hands out very seriously as she set the fruit salad carefully in them.

Just because it shouldn't hurt anything for the fruit salad to be turned upside down didn't mean she wanted him to test that theory.

"Benjamin, can you help me with this?" she asked as she held out the container with the rolls she'd made.

His smile was huge as he held his hands out, and she placed it in them.

"And, Adam, this is really heavy, but I think you can handle it." She handed him the Jell-O salad container. "Be careful not to drop it, okay?"

"Yes, ma'am," Adam said very seriously.

"I want to carry something," Daniel said, looking up at her sadly, like she forgot about him.

"I was hoping you would," she said reaching for the bag where she packed all of their extra clothes. She wasn't going to make the boys change out of their good clothes, and they were dressed down this morning for church anyway, not wearing their very best. But she figured they'd all be dirty, and possibly wet, and she packed extra things just in case. Mostly for her, because if she got wet or dirty, she knew she'd want to change, but also for the boys.

When they were going to something like this, a person never knew what was going to happen.

"Do you think you can carry this? Or is it too heavy?"

Daniel held his hand out, and said, "I can do it!"

"I thought you could," she said, ruffling his hair and smiling.

"What do I get to carry?" Armstrong said, a little bit of humor in his voice and something else in his eyes that she wasn't sure about.

"We're giving your ribs a rest, remember?" She smiled at him, picking up the casserole she had placed in it's insulated wrapper and turning toward the door. "Plus, you're driving us there, right?"

"I am, but I still feel like I ought to be doing something. Everybody else has a job."

"You can open the doors for us," Glory said, laughing at him a little because he deliberately had a little whine in his voice.

But she supposed it was something in his tone, maybe something that said he felt like he should be doing more and was a little upset that he couldn't.

It was a manly pride thing, probably.

He opened the door, and they filed out, everyone stowing their stuff in the pickup and getting in.

The boys chattered during the drive there, excited about the big hog roast and all the games and seeing their friends and having fun at church.

Armstrong didn't say much, just answered direct questions and giving the occasional smile. Glory talked with the kids and hoped that Armstrong wasn't over doing it. Maybe she should have driven separately.

They pulled into the parking lot, and the scent of roasting meat filled the cab even though the windows weren't down.

"I think they'd get a lot more people to come to church if it smelled like this every week," Armstrong said, a little under his breath as the children chattered behind them. Glory looked over and grinned.

"I'm sure that's probably the point," she said, stating the obvious.

The entire town of Sweet Water would be there today, even people from neighboring towns, and several other churches had canceled their services just to attend.

When they got out, they were met by Glory's sisters, who had come to help her carry her things.

All they ended up doing was to make sure the boys got out without spilling anything. Orchid and Lavender helped them walk over, setting things where they belonged, and then taking the boys to their classes.

"It was awfully nice of you to donate a hog for the hog roast," Glory said, sniffing the air and smiling at her sister Rose.

"It's kind of funny that we didn't even need a hog. And we ended up with one and all those piglets. It turned out to be a good thing so the least we could do was donate a couple to the church and share our good fortune," Rose said, her eyes sparkling. Giving things to others always made a person feel good.

"Well, I hope you guys fall into a sow with piglets more often. It's pretty nice of you to spread the good cheer around."

"And how are you doing?" Rose asked, as Armstrong came around the truck, slowly, but walking the best he had since his accident.

"Pretty good today. I brought pain pills along, because I figured if it weren't for your sister, I'm not sure I'd be here. She's treated me pretty well."

Rose grunted a laugh, and Glory shifted a little uncomfortably at the look in Rose's eyes. She could see where that was going in Rose's mind, and, while Glory couldn't say that she wasn't attracted to Armstrong, and wouldn't be opposed if things progressed in that direction, she was pretty sure he didn't and wasn't interested.

Just because of some of the comments he made, not anything that insulted his ex, but more along the lines of him not wanting to go through that again. Just a few times after the kids had been in bed and in passing.

Regardless, he gave her the impression that he wasn't the slightest bit interested in any kind of romance, and she had to respect them.

So she shut her sister down.

Before she could even open her mouth again.

"Would you mind carrying this casserole for me please? I had a couple of things I wanted to talk to Armstrong about having to do with the children before we separated and I don't get to see him again."

"Sure. If you guys need some privacy, just say so. You don't have to make up some kind of excuse about things you have to talk about," Rose said, putting a little emphasis on "talk" that made it clear she didn't think they were going to be doing any talking at all.

Glory wanted to shove her sister away, and give her a good swift kick in the pants while she was leaving.

"I'm sorry," she said immediately when Rose started walking away, and she looked at Armstrong.

"About what?" he said, truly looking perplexed.

She didn't know whether to explain, and embarrass herself even more, or to just assume that he truly didn't know what she was talking about and just let it go.

She decided on the second.

"Never mind. I wanted to say that the bag Daniel carried had extra clothes in it, and I packed some for you as well, just in case you need them."

He chuckled, grimacing a little, and she figured laughing probably still hurt. Unfortunately, because she hated the idea that something that was so much fun would cause pain.

"Sounds like you've been to these things a few times. But I can't imagine that anything would happen where I would need to change. I appreciate you thinking about me, though. And I'll keep that in mind about the boys. I know they'd be really disappointed if they had to be told no because someone didn't want them to get their clothes dirty."

"Exactly. That's what I'm saying. They can do whatever they want to, we're prepared."

"You know," he seemed a little uncomfortable, his fingers tightening on the side mirror of the truck where they rested. "When I complimented you to your sister, it was true. Blanche wouldn't have wanted to do that extra work in order for the kids to have a good time. And I appreciate you being willing. I appreciate all the things you've done, and the good attitude and the sunshine you've brought into my home."

Sounding a little uncomfortable, he shifted like he wasn't used to saying kind things, but he wanted to make sure he told her.

"I think this is where I ask for a raise," she joked, wanting to break the tension that seemed to have enveloped them.

But his face tightened, and the humorous look left his eyes.

Maybe he didn't like to joke about money.

Or... Maybe he had trouble, as she did, remembering that she wasn't doing this because they were a couple, but because she owed him.

"I'm sorry. I shouldn't have said that," she said immediately.

"What? There wasn't anything wrong with it. You can say whatever you want to. You don't have to apologize for it." He jerked his head toward the picnic tables, where there was a group of men standing around two large hog roasters. "I'm going to go see if there's anything I can do to help."

He probably knew as well as she did that he wouldn't be helping, but would just be standing with a group of men yakking.

She shook her head, sucking down the disappointment she felt.

He had been saying something kind, and she'd ended up throwing it in his face that she was only there because she had to be.

That wasn't how she felt.

He complemented her...she should have done the same instead of letting something stupid come out of her mouth.

Regardless, it was too late to try to fix it, even if she knew how, as he was already walking away.

Irritated with herself, she turned, heading toward the church and determined that she wasn't going to make that mistake again.

Chapter 15

My Dad's favorite saying was "Be quick to forgive and don't take offense." This has worked very well in our marriage the last 44 years.
- Joy Helmuth from Coweta, OK

Armstrong strode, carefully, toward the men who stood around the hog roasters.

Of course Glory was only doing everything she was doing because he was paying her.

She was just doing a good job. That's what he needed to say. *You did a good job.* Not a whole bunch of stupid stuff about how amazing she was and how she lit up his house with sunshine.

He couldn't even believe he'd said that. Who talked about sunshine?

"Armstrong. It's good to see you. I wasn't sure you'd make it today," Miss Charlene said, surprising Armstrong since he hadn't seen her, almost like she'd been hiding behind a car just waiting to jump out and catch him.

Miss Vicki and Miss Kathy were beside her, and Armstrong figured he was probably in trouble.

"What did I do?"

"What in the world makes you think you did something?" Miss Vicky said, with far more innocence than Armstrong felt was appropriate.

"Just a feeling I had," he said, with more than a little sarcasm in his voice.

"We just want to chat with you for a couple of minutes. Do you have time?" Miss Vicky slipped her arm into his, and gently turned him, while Miss Kathy slid her arm through on the other side and he felt like he was being led to the gallows. Like they were afraid he might try to struggle to get away, so they wanted to keep ahold of him.

Miss Charlene led the way to a spot in the parking lot where there weren't any people close.

"How are things going?" Miss Charlene asked as they stopped, and she turned to look at him.

For being older ladies, they sure got around well.

"My ribs are feeling good. As long as you don't grab a hold of me and drag me all across tarnation, I'll probably make it the whole day."

"We were gentle with you. On purpose," Kathy said, patting his arm.

He lifted a brow, then one side of his mouth pulled back. Waiting. They had something they wanted to say.

"We can't help but notice how good you and Glory look together. And very comfortable. Is everything going well?"

She ended with a question she'd already asked. He'd already answered, and he'd deliberately changed the subject and talked about his ribs.

He didn't want to talk about Glory. That felt private.

But the ladies want to help you.

He wasn't sure he wanted helped. He'd already been down that road.

Glory is not anything like Blanche.

He knew it. Still, he knew what it felt like to trust someone, and have them rip his entire world out from underneath him.

Not good.

"We just wanted to recommend to you that you be nice to her."

His head jerked up, and his mouth opened immediately. "What do you mean? I am nice." He couldn't believe they were accusing him of not being nice.

"No." Vicki patted his arm. "Calm down. We're not saying that you're not nice to her, but we want you to be *nice* to her," Miss Vicki said, her emphasis on the word "nice" making it sound like there was some kind of difference between the two of them.

"I guess you're going to have to help me. I don't understand the nuances there."

"That's why we're here, Honey," Charlene said, patting his arm like he was two.

"You guys are going to make me feel like it's my fault that my wife left," he said. He wasn't even sure what made those words come out of his mouth.

He supposed, deep in his heart, even though he knew when someone makes vows they should keep them, that it was still his fault. He hadn't been something she needed, but he didn't know what it was. Maybe there was more than one thing he hadn't been.

He should be happy they were trying to help him.

But, he'd already "caught" one woman. It was the keeping he had problems with. Obviously.

"All right. Tell me what I need to do," he said, kind of resigned, and figuring they could talk all they wanted to, but he didn't have to do what they said.

"That's not the attitude we want." Kathy said, chiding him a little.

"I guess I just don't understand what the problem is. She's helping me with the kids, I'm paying her. I'm being nice to her. Maybe not the way you think I should, but as nice as I can be."

"It's fine. And you've been in a lot of pain, so you're excused. But there are a few things you need to do. We're going to help you see them." Charlene lowered her chin slightly as she looked at him from under her brows. The kind of look his mom might have given him if he'd colored on the kitchen floor.

He waited.

"You have to be nice to her."

That's the second time they said that. "What do you mean by nice?" He was unable to keep the frustration out of his voice.

"You can't be afraid to let her know that you're thinking about her."

"I'm not afraid," he said, and even he could tell he sounded like a ten-year-old.

Charlene heard the tone too and smiled like she might smile at a ten-year-old. "Of course," she placated him.

"Let her know you're thinking about her." Miss Kathy looked at him eagerly as though she'd just given him some kind of key.

"How do you guys even know that she wants me to think about her? Maybe she can't wait until she's done helping me and can go back to her real life."

"That's your job. You're supposed to make her fall in love with you, so she won't *want* to go back to her real life."

"You guys don't care what she wants right now?"

"Of course we do. We have both of your happiness in mind. But we want to prove you'll be happy together. And you'll be together if you can manage to be nice."

Armstrong stared at the ladies, Vicki and Kathy had unclasped his arm, and they stood in a semicircle in front of him, almost like it they were ganging up on him three against one.

"I'm supposed to let her know I'm thinking about her. What am I supposed to think?" He was only being a little bit belligerent. He really didn't know.

He thought about her, sure. Her lips. For one. Her smile. The graceful way she moved, and the way she brightened up the room. Her gentle way with the children, and the way she made each of them feel important too. The way she made him feel.

"You need to appreciate her. Thank her. Let her know you notice what she's doing." He'd tried to do that today and ended up feeling stupid.

"I think she knows," he said.

"Oh honey, that's a fatal mistake. You can't assume that a woman knows what you're thinking. How in the world are they supposed to know? Is it written on your forehead?"

"No. It just makes sense. If I'm there, I'm happy. She can figure that out." Couldn't she? She knew he appreciated her. She knew he was happy with her. She probably knew he liked her, too, which is why she did that whole just working for you thing today.

Right?

"No. You have to say something. You can't just assume that a woman knows you want her, or that you appreciate her, or that you admire her. You have to tell her," Charlene explained.

"And then you have to show her," Vicki said.

Kathy nodded in agreement.

"Actions are probably more important than words."

"How do I show I appreciate her?" He was baffled. Wasn't that why he said "thank you?"

"Do something nice for her. Do it. Don't just say it. Words are easy."

"Although, use words too," Kathy said immediately.

"I guess this is why I'm not married anymore. This all feels very complicated. Do, say, show and I don't even know what I'm doing and saying and showing. I just know I like her. I figure she probably knows, and there isn't too much else more I need to do, since she doesn't seem to like me."

"She does like you! That's the whole reason we're here," Charlene said, like that should have been obvious from the beginning

"How do you know? Did she tell you?"

"She doesn't have to tell us. We can tell by the way she looks. And what she says about you. By the way she admires you."

"How do you know she's admiring me? And why don't I know that?

"You just have to open up your eyes and see. Look at how she looks. Do you think she'd be looking like that at some other man?"

"I don't know," Armstrong said, feeling like this whole conversation had been like walking through knee-deep mud. It was murky and he had to fight in his mind to try to make sense of what they were saying, because apparently what he was doing wasn't what they were saying, although he thought he'd been doing a pretty good job.

"Armstrong. Have you asked her out?" Vicki asked.

"No. I've barely been able to walk."

"Have you told her that when you can walk you want to ask her out?" Kathy prompted.

"No. I want her to be working for me until I can at least take care of myself. I don't want to scare her away."

"Telling her you're interested in her is not going to scare her away. Where did you ever get that idea?" Charlene asked, sounded like the concept was very elementary, and he just flunked the simplest test in the world.

"She doesn't want my attention."

"But she does want it. That's the thing."

"Maybe you need to talk to her. After the kids go to bed, ask her to spend some time with you. You guys can take a walk together. Do you ever do anything without the children?"

"Sure. We fed the stock together without kids."

"Anything that is not working," Kathy clarified, and he got the impression that she really wanted to roll her eyes but was containing herself.

"I think working together counts. We're spending time together." That seemed reasonable to him.

"Okay. Working together counts half. When you have a chance to do things other than working, you have to act like you want to spend time with her. That makes her feel like you care. You have to act like you want to look at her. Act like you want to be with her. Show her by seeking her out. Maybe you can do some little things."

He couldn't keep up with all of the work that he had to do for himself. Now they wanted him to do her jobs too? He thought that's what they were saying, and he was certainly willing to do all of her jobs, but then what was the point in hiring her?

He was confused. But he knew one thing. "I understand now why I'm not married anymore. This is all way too confusing and I really don't even have an idea of what you ladies are talking about."

They all stared at him like there was something wrong with him. He felt like there was. He was broken somehow where he didn't have whatever it was that men needed in order to do whatever it was that women needed them to do, in order for a woman to want to stay with a man.

Now he wasn't even making sense.

Charlene crossed her arms over her chest, and she glared at him.

"It's pretty simple. Let me boil it down to the essential thing." She lifted her brows, and he lifted his right back at her, like he'd do whatever he needed to do, and didn't have a problem. He just had no idea what it was.

"You need to think about someone other than yourself. You need to be concerned about someone other than you. Putting someone else first.

Her.

Think about what she wants. Think about what she might be thinking about. Think about what you can do that will make her life easier."

"We're not calling you selfish," Vicki said, even though he was pretty sure that's exactly what they had just done. "We're just saying that it's human nature to think about ourselves. The jobs that we have to do, the work that's facing us, the things that we want, and the things that make us happy."

"What you have to do is focus on someone else, and think about what she might want. What makes her happy. What you can do, even just little things, that would make her smile. Make that your whole goal in life - to see her smile."

Armstrong nodded at the ladies, thinking that he didn't think of himself as a selfish person. Didn't think that he lived for himself, but if he thought about it, what had he done to try to make things easier for anyone?

He tried to take care of his children, but otherwise, he put his work first. Which was basically putting himself first. He didn't have much free time, and he didn't do too many things for fun, but...maybe he should start thinking about trying to do things for fun that Glory might want to do.

He'd gone to the auction just for her. But...he supposed he hadn't told her that was why he was there. He just assumed she knew.

Maybe the ladies were right. Maybe she really didn't know.

"Has she been complaining that I haven't been nice? Or that I'm selfish?" he finally asked, wondering if it had been blatantly obvious and he'd missed it.

"Oh, no!" Charlene said immediately.

"We're just trying to help you. We know you'll be happy with her. And she'll be happy with you. Everyone can see it. But, I think especially with four children and a farm to take care of, and a wife that's already left, we just figured you needed a little help. Because —"

"I'm a man," he finished her sentence for her.

"No. You don't get to hide behind your gender like that's some kind of excuse. It might be harder for you, but that's where the benefits are found – by doing something hard. That makes her realize you care. When you put the work into doing things that don't come naturally."

"Maybe you don't even realize that it's easy for everyone to see you two are perfect together," Kathy said, her tone compassionate.

"I don't know how anyone could not like Glory. She's truly an amazing woman, and one that any man would be blessed to have." He wasn't good with words, but he figured he knew what he was saying. "But after listening to you guys, I feel like maybe I shouldn't even be trying for her. She deserves someone better than me. Someone who can be...*nice*...to her."

"Everyone can use some improvement. We wouldn't be doing our jobs if we just let you go."

"I don't know if I can live up to what you ladies expect me to be. And I still feel confused, but I guess you're right. I do want to try to improve. And I suppose if I really think about it, you're right about me putting, not myself necessarily first, but the things that I want first."

He wanted someone to hear about his day, but he didn't necessarily sit around and listen to someone else's day. At least, he hadn't thought about it like that. He wanted someone to admire him, so he supposed he needed to reciprocate. In ways that she could understand. Maybe the things that he was doing weren't translating into things that showed her he cared. Not because he didn't care, but because she didn't understand that's what he was saying with the things he did.

Maybe women and men really did speak in different ways, and he'd been trying to talk like a man to the woman in his life, and it hadn't been working out.

The idea was intriguing, and something for him to think about.

"I think we got through to him," Vicki said, like he wasn't still standing there.

"I told you he wouldn't be belligerent. He's a good man," Charlene said, nodding at him like the ladies needed her to show them where he was.

"Glory is a good woman, and she deserves someone who appreciates her. Although, lots of women stay with men who don't. Or who do, but don't know how to show it."

"And that's too bad. Because I know you want to make her feel like she's the most important thing in your life. Like you admire her, and only her. Like...like you love her," Charlene added.

Did he?

He possibly might. Although the idea was shocking.

"It's time for church to start. You need to start walking back. Make sure you don't overdo it on the ribs today," Vicki said, taking his arm as she had before and turning him around.

They'd given him a lot to think about, and from the little bit he decided, he figured... They were probably right.

Chapter 16

Commitment, compromise, sacrifice, above all Jesus at the
center of your relationship.
- Terri Fleming from Adrian, GA

"The weather couldn't be better for this," Glory said as she
sat with Armstrong and the four boys on their blanket,
their lunch spread out in front of them, other families scattered
all around the church grounds.

"Sometimes it's even more fun inside," Armstrong commented
mildly. He seemed kind of quiet and contemplative. Not like he
wasn't that usually, but even more so.

She'd been on the verge several times of asking him if there was
a problem, but maybe he was just upset that he wasn't able to do
as much with his boys as he wanted to.

He hadn't been able to do the steer wrestling contest, or the hog
race.

He hadn't even done the tractor driving contest, just because he
hadn't wanted to do anything that was going to jar his ribs and keep
him from being able to work on the farm this week.

She got that, but felt bad for him, because the hog roast only
happened once a year, and she could tell it bothered him that he
wasn't getting to participate with his children like he wanted to.

The boys chattered amongst themselves, excited, because of
all the things they'd done, and all the things that were going to
happen.

Daniel sat in her lap as she sat cross legged on the ground, and she helped him eat.

Even he had been having a good time, although he seemed sleepy now. He'd missed his nap and it was going on four o'clock in the afternoon.

"That's true. I remember a few years where it rained, and they had some backup things going on inside, and with all the people and the general hubbub, it was a lot of fun."

"I remember that year too, although I haven't been able to make it every year."

She nodded but didn't say anything. He lived a long way away, and she didn't remember seeing too much of him over the years.

She thought about talking to him about what the Piece Maker ladies had talked to her about. They'd stopped her as soon as she dropped her casserole off in the kitchen and stopped to chat to a few ladies. They been waiting for her outside the kitchen.

They suggested that she consider Armstrong as more than her employer. They listed all the reasons they thought was a good idea, from her being good with his children, to them being very compatible as a couple, to him being willing to step between her and a charging cow.

They had a point with the cow.

She supposed their other points were valid too, and they'd had more. In fact, she felt like she'd been attacked by a group of lawyers rather than a group of ladies.

But now, as the boys slowly finished eating and started playing with their friends, she wondered if it would be a good time for her to bring the idea up to Armstrong.

She wasn't going to go behind his back and start trying to attract him, which is what the ladies had suggested.

If she wanted their relationship to change, she wanted to be upfront about it.

There was no better time than the present, she figured, as Daniel leaned back on her chest, his head drooping down, leaning against her.

She opened her mouth, but, before she could say anything Armstrong started talking.

"I talked to the Piece Maker ladies before I even went in the church today. Actually, they caught me before I got to the men at the hog roaster.

"That's funny," she said immediately, wondering what in the world they could have been talking to him about. "They got me as I was leaving the kitchen after dropping off my casserole.

"Really?" He looked at her curiously.

He was probably wondering the same thing she was.

Knowing they had spoken to him, too, made her not want to go first. She highly doubted that the ladies would have told her to go after Armstrong romantically, and then cautioned him not to go after her, but...what in the world had they said?

"They told me I was part of the reason my marriage blew up."

He just threw that out there, and then didn't say anything.

"Ouch."

She couldn't think of anything else to say. From what little she had heard, his wife just walked out saying she wanted to be single again. She hardly thought that that was Armstrong's fault.

"Did they tell you why?" she asked, knowing they'd come to her with a whole list of things. If they did that to her, maybe they'd done it to him too.

"Yeah. They had about seventeen reasons why."

"I see," she laughed. "I suppose they would have been better off being lawyers than quilters, because they did the same thing to me. I felt a little blind-sided as they ticked off all the reasons I should do what they were asking me to do."

"What were they asking you to do?"

She gave him a doubtful look. Not wanting to say. It might make him uncomfortable. "If I tell you, will it keep you from telling me what they told you?"

"No. I promise I'll tell you."

"Yay. A promise," she said, being a little silly, because he didn't need to promise. If he told her he was going to do it, she'd believe him.

He grinned, maybe a little embarrassed, but there was also a bit of confidence in his gaze, like he understood she accepted his word without question, and it made him feel good.

"They think you would make a good boyfriend for me." She lifted her shoulder. "That was the basic gist."

He grunted. "That's funny. Because they basically told me I wasn't good enough for you, and I didn't treat my wife well, and I need to make sure I was treating you better, although, I guess the end goal was to get you to like me, as in more than *like* me."

He looked a little sheepish saying that, like he didn't really like to talk about it, but he had promised. Her lips tilted further up. And his smile answered hers, like they were sharing a little laughter over something just the two of them got.

"So what did they say you needed to do?" she asked, shifting Daniel ever so slightly, as his eyes drooped closed. He moved but didn't wake.

"I think basically they said I needed to be more considerate, to let you know that I admire you, that I should talk to you about more than just the farm, and...I'm not even sure. But they basically said that Blanche left because I didn't make her feel loved and wanted. Which, looking back, I suppose could be true. But she wouldn't talk to me about it. I would have been more than happy to try to fix things. How can I fix things when she just leaves? Especially if I don't know there's anything wrong?"

"So maybe that was their point? They feel like you should know that there was something wrong?"

"That probably was one of them, although I don't remember specifically."

"People notice different things. I'm sure Blanche probably didn't notice when the corn was ready to harvest, and she didn't notice when it was time to plant. She probably also didn't notice when the cows needed fed, or have any idea of what she should feed them."

"That's all true."

"But she probably did notice when you were tired, and when you wanted to talk. Or when you walked in and would prefer to be left alone. She also probably knew your favorite meal and your birthday."

"I don't know about all that. Although she did know my birthday. She never forgot the kids' birthdays either, which I have a tendency to do if no one reminds me. With her out of the house, I've been keeping better track of them since there isn't anyone to remind me."

"Doesn't she call them on their birthdays or come see them or something?"

"So far, no."

Glory tried to keep the shocked look off her face. A birthday was a very basic thing to remember. For a spouse or friend, absolutely. But for a mother? The idea that a mother wouldn't at least call her child on their birthday, even if she didn't come and have a big celebration, was almost unthinkable. Everyone, but kids especially, like to have something special done on their birthday.

"Wow. I guess I understand what the ladies are saying. That if you want to have a good relationship, you have to try to think more like your partner is thinking and see things from their perspective."

"I think they said those exact words," Armstrong said with a self-effacing smile.

"That's not really something that comes naturally. Don't beat yourself up about it. You can't always get everything right. It's just human nature to want to think about yourself. To put yourself first. Your stuff, your interest, you."

"But I feel like by putting my interests first, I'm taking care of her, because my interests are what pays the bills for our family. I guess I just don't see what the problem is with me putting that first."

"Well, is the farm more important than your wife?"

"That's just it, I love the farm, that's true. But I work hard on the farm, so that I can take care of my wife because I love her." He kind of stumbled over the word love, and she assumed it was because maybe he didn't want to love Blanche anymore.

"I get that. Truly. But I don't think that that translates into showing love to a woman. You know?"

"I guess. But the things that they were saying, I just... I didn't even really understand how I could put them into practice."

"I don't know what they were saying, but everyone is different. What one woman likes, another won't."

"I know. The game is rigged against us from the beginning."

They laughed, and then they kind of lapsed into silence for a bit, until Armstrong spoke, lower and softer than what he had been.

"They're trying to do a little matchmaking between us."

"Definitely. I didn't have any questions about that I just didn't realize they were talking to you, too. They made it sound like it was all going to be on my shoulders."

"Are you okay with that?"

His words caused her stomach to flip and tighten and squeeze. Was she?

She really liked him and couldn't deny that she definitely felt attracted to him. She knew for a fact that he would be an excellent father, a hard-working husband, and if he was willing to work on things, he would make a superb husband.

"Are you?" She decided to throw the ball right back at him. That was a question she wasn't sure she could answer. Well, she could answer, but it felt risky. Like if she said yes, when he said no, everything would be awkward from there on out, and she didn't want to have to do awkward for the entire summer.

"I didn't need the ladies to tell me that you would be an excellent catch. That you would make a great wife. You're great with my kids. I didn't even need the ladies to tell me that I'm attracted to you. I maybe wondered if you might feel the same. But, they kind of scared me with all the things they said I was doing wrong."

His breath blew out and he looked away, before he rested his hand on his knees and stared at it.

"I just know I can't do all that. It's not that I don't want to try. I will. I just...I've already had one woman walk out on me, and honestly I had no idea it was going to happen, had no idea she was unhappy. I'm afraid...well, afraid the ladies are right. You deserve someone better than me. I'm willing to try to work to improve, but I don't know that I would ever be what you deserve."

She loved the humbleness, the lack of arrogance or pride. The fact that he was willing to admit there might be fault, and he would work on anything he needed to, showed her that along with being everything she already knew he was, he was also a man who would be, if not easy to get along with, someone who would work on their problems rather than retreating into silence and anger.

"I'm not sure exactly whether that was a yes or no to my question, but it gave me the confidence to feel like I can say that I'm definitely interested in their suggestion. It might be a little bit touchy since I'm working for you, and watching your children, and it already feels a little bit like we're family, sitting here on the blanket together. But, maybe that's a good thing. I like the way it feels. And...I like being with you."

He grinned, and maybe that grin was a little bit cocky. Just because her words made him happy.

"That's a good thing. Because I ended up at the auction last night because I didn't want to be sitting around at home without you. It didn't feel right with you not being there. Already I want to be where you are, which makes me feel like I've reverted back to my teenage years, and can't live without you."

"I don't know what the ladies told you, but I think that kind of attention makes a woman feel good. The idea that the man she's interested in is thinking about her, and wants to be with her, and will go out of his way to do something that isn't easy in order just to see her."

That was a major understatement. For her anyway. She supposed other ladies enjoyed getting flowers, or gifts, or maybe even having all the pretty words. That had never been her.

She wanted to see the actions. The effort. To see that he truly was thinking about her. That he didn't want to go all evening without being with her was a big thing in her book.

Daniel stirred a little, and she took the opportunity to lay him down. He curled up on the blanket, thumb in his mouth, hand under his chin, and never opened his eyes.

"I don't think I could have gotten him to do that. He would have been fussy all afternoon, and I'd have wished we were home so I could put him to bed. I might have made the kids leave early."

"That's fine. There is no law that says that he has to sleep here. Or that he has to sleep at all. Sometimes kids are just fussy at these things."

Armstrong didn't get a chance to reply, because the calmness of the air was suddenly shattered by the shrill ringing of the cowbell.

Action started everywhere, as Glory jumped to her feet, looking to make sure Armstrong was going to be keeping an eye on Daniel.

At his abrupt nod, she ran to Adam, who had been searching for her, and they grabbed hands.

They'd made their plans ahead of time, after the rules had been announced.

Although they really didn't need to hear it, because this happened every year.

Sometime during the sit down meal, the cowbell would go off and there was a race around the church. Teams consisted of one adult and one child. The first one to make it the entire way around and jump in the watering trough that was set up exactly for that purpose, would win an entire five pound bag of candy.

Adam, Benjamin, and Caleb had taken one look at the bag of candy and had made a plan in order to try to win it.

Glory had been a part of that plan. The strategic positioning of the blanket had been another part of that plan.

They had put it as close to the church as possible.

Now, she and Adam ran around the building, easily in the lead.

"I think we can win!" Adam yelled, looking over at her as they ran.

"Focus on running as fast as you can. We'll celebrate after we win," she shouted back at him. Knowing that if they were going to lose now, it would probably be a stupid mistake on their part. There might be kids who could outrun them, but there wasn't anyone close enough who could catch up to them.

They made it around the last corner of the church and charged toward the watering trough.

As Glory was jumping, about to land in the water, she realized she really hadn't thought this through.

She didn't want to get wet.

It was too late, and she and Adam crashed into the water with a huge splash. As they sat up, laughing and hugging each other, there were cheers all around.

Benjamin and Caleb came over, dancing up and down, and talking about the kinds of candy they had seen in the five pound bag.

Glory had a second epiphany as she realized it was going to be her job to watch the children as they eat the five pound bag of candy.

She definitely needed to teach the benefits of rationing.

But she wasn't going to worry about that now. It was just such a joy to see the kids so happy, it didn't even really matter that she was completely drenched from head to toe as she waited for Adam to get out of the watering trough, and then she threw her own leg over.

"Hey, look up, I want to take a picture," Rose said, as Glory had gotten one foot over the edge and was in the process of bringing her other one over.

All the splashing water had made the ground around the trough muddy, and her foot slipped out from underneath her. She landed in a puddle of mud, her entire front covered with the stuff, and the muddy water splashing into her face.

She figured she was probably going to make the front page of wherever Rose was going to be posting those pictures.

She didn't care. The kids were excited and having a good time, and if that meant she was going to be wet and covered in mud, then it was worth it.

After everything they'd been through, she was happy to see Adam was actually loosening up and had lost his serious demeanor, even if it was just for a little while.

Someone handed her a fistfull of paper towels, and she was able to get her face wiped off, as the boys jumped and chattered around her and they made their way back to the blanket.

All the excitement had woken Daniel up, and he was sitting in Armstrong's lap as they walked toward the blanket.

Glory smiled at the little boy. He rubbed his eyes slightly, and at first she didn't notice the woman who had sat down on the blanket beside Armstrong where Glory had been sitting before she jumped up to run around the church.

But then she did, and her smile seemed to freeze on her face.

The woman was beautiful, maybe not cover model beautiful, but her hair was long and wavy and looked a lot like she just stepped out of the salon.

Her makeup was perfect, accenting her deep brown eyes, and her flawless golden skin.

With her back straight and her red cowboy boots propped in front of her, she sat on slim hips, her waist curving in.

She looked too young and beautiful to have had four children, but Glory was pretty sure that she was looking at Blanche, Armstrong's ex wife.

Chapter 17

Commitment and trust along with putting God in the marriage is what makes a Marriage last. Without God being the head of the marriage, it is difficult to have trust an commitment.
- Valerie Allard from San Pedro Sula, Honduras

B lanche sure had terrible timing.

She hadn't gotten any better since she walked out the door. She'd walked in the summer of course. When all four kids were home from school, and he had a boatload of work to do every day.

Now, he'd just talked to Glory about their relationship, felt like they might be getting somewhere and Blanche sidles up and plops down like she belonged beside him still.

They were divorced. The papers were signed. She didn't belong beside him. Not anymore.

It had been her choice.

But he wasn't going back down that road again.

She hadn't really asked. She'd just murmured, "Hi Armstrong," like it had been yesterday since they'd last spoken, and then she sat down.

He wasn't sure if she chose a spot because it was behind Daniel, and he wouldn't see her, or if she'd just chosen the spot because she'd been watching and knew that was where Glory had been sitting.

He really didn't know how long she'd been there. He hadn't seen her pull in – hadn't known she was coming at all.

But he didn't get a chance to talk to her about it, because people had started screaming and cheering, and he couldn't help but smile as he realized that Glory and Adam had won.

He wished he had been able to do it with Adam, because Adam had actually been acting like a little kid about it - wanting to win candy, being excited, smiling and chattering.

Instead of the little adult he usually acted like.

Not that there was anything wrong with the child acting like an adult. That was his personality, and it was fine.

He just supposed every parent wanted their children to have a fun and happy childhood. And Adam always seemed so serious.

He hadn't really been that way until his mom had left.

"Is there a reason you're here?" he asked as Daniel woke up because of all the noise and crawled into his lap without ever looking behind him, not realizing his mother sat so close.

"Of course. These are my children too." Blanche's words held a certain amount of censure, like he shouldn't be questioning her about whether or not she wanted to spend time with her children.

"It's nice that you remember that now. Last summer you seemed to forget."

"Really? We have to go there? Can't you just act like an adult for once?" Blanche said, her voice condescending, and her gaze giving him no doubt as to what she thought about him.

At least it was a relief to know that she wasn't here trying to get him back. That would make things awkward between Glory and him, and he didn't want that.

He had been nervous, his hands sweating, his heart pounding, as they'd been talking about whether or not they should be more than friends - whether they should pursue a romantic relationship.

He hadn't wanted her to know how very badly he wanted it. How it had been all he'd thought about since the Piece Makers had talked to him.

How he'd thought about it before, but thought it was out of his reach.

Although, when he told her that he wasn't sure he was good enough, he was just being honest with her. He truly didn't know. Didn't know if he had what it took to make a woman happy. To keep her happy. To give her what she needed and have the honor of spending a lifetime with her.

Plus he had four children. Wouldn't a woman have to be crazy to step into a family like that?

But, if he actually did have a chance, he wasn't going to let Blanche ruin it. Didn't want to, anyway.

He turned his eyes away, and looked down toward the watering trough where the crowd was now dispersing.

He smiled as Glory walked toward him, surrounded by his boys, who were chattering and jumping and surely telling her how awesome it was that they'd won the candy.

Maybe they were trying to figure out how they were going to divide it up. That would probably take the rest of the afternoon to figure out how to do that.

And they hadn't even gotten the bag yet.

Somehow Glory had gotten mud all over her, although he'd missed it. Maybe she fell down getting out of the water trough.

That made sense, since it was probably muddy and slippery.

Regardless, she was laughing and chattering with the boys, and it didn't matter how much mud she had on her, how wet her hair was, or whatever other things concerned a woman, it didn't bother him at all. In fact, it made her more appealing. That she wasn't afraid to get wet, or dirty, especially not just for work, but just to make his boys smile.

They weren't hers, she didn't have anything invested in them, but it showed her good and generous nature that she would care about them so much that she would be willing to go to such lengths to make them smile.

She looked up, and he was hoping to meet her gaze, to let her know how much he appreciated what she'd done, just seeing his boys so happy, seeing her laughing with them.

Them all having a good time together was worth so much more to him than anything else she could have done.

But, her gaze went first to Daniel, maybe checking to make sure he was okay, and then it slid to Blanche.

It took a couple of seconds, but he could tell the instant she realized he was sitting beside his ex-wife.

Her smile was still there, but the spirit behind it died.

He hated that. Hated the fact that he couldn't do anything about it, either.

He could hardly kick Blanche away, since she claimed to be there to see the boys.

Maybe he could get up.

The thought had barely formed in his head before he did that very thing, lifting Daniel up with him, and grimacing as the movement hurt his ribs.

"Daddy! Daddy! Did you see us? We won! We got the big bag of candy," Adam said, rushing to his dad, soaking wet, but smiling from ear to ear.

Armstrong didn't even care that his child was wet, and he ignored the pain in his ribs as Adam wrapped his arms around him and hugged him tight in his excitement.

He couldn't remember the last time Adam had been this excited, but it definitely been before Blanche had left.

The boys gathered around him, each of them trying to talk over top of each other, and he paid attention to them, or tried to, although he looked up several times, trying to meet Glory's eyes.

She stood there for a minute, and then she walked over and held her hand out to Blanche.

"I'm Glory. And you must be Blanche."

"If you don't mind, you look kind of muddy. I think I'll wait until you get cleaned up to shake your hand, but thanks anyway," Blanche said, in a very kind, almost condescending tone.

Glory's eyebrows moved and her hand dropped.

"That's a good idea. I guess I'll do that."

She walked away, and never did look at him.

It was almost like he had imagined the entire conversation that they had just before she jumped up, laughing and running with Adam.

Like it had never happened.

But he supposed if her ex had shown up, sitting down on a blanket beside her looking all cozy, he might feel a little insecure about that too.

"Aren't you going to have your boys say hi to their mother?" Blanche said, and he realized that while he'd been watching Glory walk away, Blanche had stood up.

At the sound of her voice, his boys had quieted, and now they turned toward her.

Armstrong was actually a little surprised they hadn't seen her to begin with, but he supposed five pounds of candy could turn any boy's head.

The kids quieted and their mouths opened as they saw her and recognized her, their eyes bugging out.

Daniel was the first to react. He screamed and threw his body at his mother, his arms going out as he screamed her name.

It was such a heartbreaking show of absolute love. Despite the fact that she had been gone for months, little Daniel loved her anyway.

Benjamin and Caleb acted the exact same way, screaming and throwing themselves at Blanche, who looked annoyed, but still wrapped her arms around them.

Armstrong couldn't help but have the verse go through his head that talked about suffering the little children to come unto Jesus and forbid them not, for of such is the kingdom of heaven.

And the one that said in order to get to heaven one had to become like a little child.

Innocent.

Trusting.

Forgiving.

Armstrong wished he could forgive as easily. That's what God asked of him.

Blind faith like Daniel had that his mother had come back and she wouldn't leave again. Blind love that didn't see the chasm that had been created when she left and only saw that she was back.

Like the father's love for a prodigal son.

That's what Benjamin, Caleb and Daniel showed to their mother right now.

Adam was a little standoffish.

His look wasn't nearly as trusting. In fact he looked downright suspicious.

But, there was a sadness in his eyes, almost a longing, and it broke Armstrong's heart almost as much as Daniel's absolute eagerness to be with Blanche.

It also made him angry. Angry at what she had done to his children, to their family. The pain that she had caused, and how she just waltzed back in and expected everything to be okay.

The gentle prodding that he needed to forgive pushed in the back of his head, but he shoved it aside, anger taking its place. He wasn't ready to forgive.

She didn't deserve forgiveness. She hadn't even asked for it. She was acting like she hadn't even done anything wrong.

If she had come, contrite, apologetically, acting kindly toward Glory and humble toward him, he would have struggled to forgive her, but it would have been easier. Maybe he would have done it.

But she wasn't acting like that at all. She was acting like she owned the place, like she deserved the spot she occupied right now. Deserved the children's love and adoration.

When he knew she didn't.

Which is right? The way Daniel acted, or the way you are acting?

That simple question floated into his head. He wanted to shove that aside as well, but it was a good question, and one he needed to ask himself.

After all, the answer was obvious. Daniel was acting the way he should be acting. Forgiving the way Jesus forgives. Forgiving the way God had forgiven him when Jesus paid for his sin.

Forgiveness requires pain. Forgiveness means that you racked up the debt, and I'll pay it. I'll take the pain, cover the cost, and you go free.

He knew that was what forgiveness was, and that was what was so difficult about it. He didn't want Blanche to go free. He didn't want to pay for it for her.

And it wasn't just his pain. It was his children's pain too. He had to see their pain, their tears, their hardship, and pay for that too.

God, it's too much! Too much to ask of anyone!

Freely have you received. Freely give.

He didn't want to. He really didn't want to.

"So are you boys ready to go back to our house? We'll have supper together, and I'll stay there tonight, and we'll all go to your school's field day tomorrow."

"How did you know about field day?"

"Don't you read the emails the school sends home?" she asked, with her brows raised and that slightly snobby tone in her voice that said that he was not a good parent.

The tone she normally used when she talked to him before she left.

He wanted to say yes, but that would be a lie. He tried to keep up. But he didn't always read every single one. It seemed like they sent three home every day.

The boys were screaming and jumping up and down, and at some point Benjamin had turned to him and said, "It's okay, right Daddy? Mommy can come home with us! She can live with us again!"

Armstrong's eyes lifted from the excited face of his son to the smug look of his ex-wife.

He kept his own expression as impassive as possible, knowing that he had to get through this somehow. But she was not going to live in his house.

"I was thinking about doing the very thing, Ben. About how it would be nice for us to come back and live together as a family."

She gave Caleb a fake squeezy smile, the kind of smile that an adult who is not very good with children gives to a child. One that a child of Adam's age could tell was fake from the get-go.

"I thought Glory was going to stay," Adam said, and all the joy and excitement of winning the race was completely gone. He didn't like the fact that his mother was home, and Armstrong figured he probably felt about the same way Armstrong did.

"If your mother is back, you don't need me," Glory said, walking up to the blanket, a smile on her face, but it didn't quite hide the clouds in her eyes.

Not to mention, she didn't look at him.

"She's not staying. And yes. We need you." Armstrong spoke immediately, not wanting Glory to get the wrong idea, and not wanting her to leave again without him being able to say something. He wouldn't let her. He'd chase after her if necessary.

Her hair was still wet, but she had on a clean pair of jeans, and a pink T-shirt, which brought out the color of her face and the brightness of her eyes.

"No really, we don't need you. Although if you want to come and help cook and clean, I'm sure we can settle on a day for you to do that," Blanche said, like Armstrong hadn't spoken.

"We can talk about this later, Blanche." Maybe he was being too harsh. But, she was the one who had moved out. She'd made her choice. He wasn't letting her come back and act like nothing had happened.

"Are you serious?" Her eyes narrowed, and she lowered her head. Like he was being completely unreasonable. "The nearest hotel is thirty miles away. It'll take me an hour to get to the school in the morning if I don't stay here."

"I guess you should have thought of that before you drove here without calling. I'll allow you in the house, because you're the children's mother, and if you want a relationship with them, I'm happy about that. But I'm not going to support you just moving in and out of my house on a whim. We've already done that. You had your chance to be a family. Now your chance is gone."

Her lips tightened, and her eyes narrowed, and then she turned her gaze toward Glory.

"Would you mind watching the children for a moment please?" She gave a tight smile that was obviously fake. "I need to talk to Armstrong."

"Of course. You guys can go ahead and do whatever you want. The games are going to be starting soon, and I'll be with the kids."

Her voice was friendly, but there was something else in it he couldn't identify, and he knew he could have handled things a little better. At least, he could have been more clear about what he wanted.

So be more clear.

He almost laughed at the voice, and then he changed his mind. All right. He would.

He swallowed, walked around the blanket until he stood in front of Glory. But he didn't stop there. He wrapped his hands around her upper arms, and then changed his mind. Sliding his hands around her back, one going to the small of her back, one around her shoulders, he pulled her close, but not tight.

"Sorry. I didn't know she was coming. And I don't want her to stay. I'm trying to act like an adult, as much as I want her to leave and never come back."

When Glory's eyes lifted to his, he could see the there was still pain there. But she smiled sadly, as her arms lifted and went around his neck.

"I love that you're doing the adult thing. That you're trying to do what's best for the children. That's really a lot more than most people try to do. And that's what's best for them. That's what I want too." Concern and compassion filled her tone.

"I want you."

That didn't come out the way he meant, exactly, although he didn't know exactly what he was trying to say. Just that...that he wanted the children and her. And he didn't want Blanche. But he'd put up with Blanche if he had to, because that was the right thing to do.

"I guess I'm trying to say, I have to allow Blanche to stay, but I want you." He lifted his brows and knew there was pleading on his face, wanting her to understand.

Her smile said she did. He shivered as her fingers ran through the short hairs at the base of his head. "Thank you. That's what I needed to hear."

Chapter 18

Spending quality time together and finding out what your
spouse loves and then doing that for them.
- Karen from California

Armstrong stood with a group of men waiting for the ladies to finish putting the leftover pork away before they cleaned up the hog cookers.

Two of his brothers, Calhoun and Nolt, stood with him and listened to Rem Hernandez talking about the cabins he rented around the lake that were on the property that he owned with his wife Elaine and their eight children.

"It's a beautiful place, but I hadn't realized it had gotten so popular," Nolt said, one hand in his pocket, the other hanging loosely at his side as he looked thoughtfully at Rem.

"It shocked me too. Just in the last few years it's started to boom. Elaine and I can hardly keep up. Thankfully, the older kids help us keep things cleaned. Although a few times we've had to scramble when they had the typical teen stuff going on."

Armstrong and his brothers nodded all along with Rem, although none of them really knew what typical teen stuff was. Other than from experience during their own teenage years.

"I think that's such a good thing for our local economy, although it's not really going to affect our trucking business much, or our feed mill." Calhoun, who was known as the goofball in the family, sometimes hid his intelligence behind humor, but he seemed extra serious today. Armstrong figured maybe if he didn't have his head so far in his own problems, he might find that Calhoun had found someone he might be interested in. Maybe she was here with someone else. That would explain his lack of goofiness.

"I doubt Glory and her family will see much in the way of any increase in business either, but the diner should be busier. Although that might be too small for some of the rich ticks who've booked."

"We do have some normal people in. Really nice folks. A lot of them are just here to get away. Since it's so remote, and so isolated, and so pretty, it's just a really great place to unplug."

Rem had his arms crossed over his chest and his feet braced. "Although we actually have a Hollywood celebrity who's coming in over Christmas who booked the entire place. Every cabin."

"They're bringing an entire crew and with them?" Nolt asked, interested.

"No. I don't think so. I think it's just one person; they just want extreme privacy. At least that's what we understood from their booking agent. We didn't actually talk to a real celebrity or anything. Elaine took the call."

Rem was probably in his mid-forties. He sometimes walked with a limp, probably the aggravation of an old injury from his bull riding days.

His dark hair was laced with silver, but when his eyes fell on his wife, who was over working with Glory, they softened, and he looked almost young. Definitely like a man who was still in love.

The conversation flowed around him, but Armstrong had followed Rem's gaze over to the group of ladies who were working.

Elaine, her blonde hair streaked with white, and her once slender figure looking a little more matronly than it had, at least that Armstrong remembered growing up, still had a soft smile, gentle movements, and kindness that seemed to radiate from her. None of that had changed.

Armstrong wasn't fooled, though. Elaine looked almost ethereal but she was North Dakota tough.

His gaze shifted to Glory, who was laughing at something Elaine had said. North Dakota tough the same as Glory.

Not tough in a manly kind of way, but tough in that resilient, but still gracious and kind way a woman had sometimes.

Glory had it.

The things that the Piece Maker ladies had said came back to him, and he wondered if they were even right.

Did she need all of that special stuff? Fancy dates and dinners, gifts of jewelry and flowers?

It just didn't seem like Glory. They just didn't seem like things that would mean anything to her or that she would want. He tried to imagine her in fancy dress, and just couldn't.

As he watched, Benjamin came over, tapping her on the side to get her attention.

Far from looking irritated she looked down with a smile and chatted with him, then handed him a container, and seemed to be giving him a job.

He looked proud to be helping, and Glory seemed to say something to Elaine, who looked at Benjamin with a smile, maybe praising him for doing a great job.

Benjamin beamed.

Just watching the interaction warmed Armstrong's heart and did something funny to his chest. Seeing his son so happy, seeing someone who obviously wasn't doing it for show, because she didn't know he was watching. She wasn't doing it for the accolades, or to impress anyone.

She just loved his kid and cared about him.

She was exactly the kind of person that he'd want to watch his children, but...he wanted more.

As he thought about that, he remembered Blanche and looked around for her.

He didn't have to look far, since she was sitting not far from the spot where the ladies were working, relaxing in a chair in the shade. Daniel was plastered to her, clinging tightly, and she seemed annoyed.

It had gotten rather warm, and he supposed holding the child probably made her hot. Daniel had spent the day outside and he was grubby as well, and she seemed to lean away from him some, like she didn't want to get dirty, either.

Caleb stood beside her, his hand on her shoulder. As Armstrong watched, the hand went to her hair, like he just wanted to run his fingers through it, and she shoved his hand away, maybe not wanting her hair messed up, or maybe not wanting it to get dirty. He wasn't sure, just knew she didn't want her child touching her hair.

It reminded Armstrong of the times she'd pushed him away.

He hadn't really understood why, just that she seemed moody, and didn't always want attention or affection. At least from him.

Which made him wonder, why was she back? She couldn't want to get back together with him. She'd been pretty clear about what she thought about living on a farm and with a family and kids.

Even though he hadn't made any bones about what he wanted to be when they got married. Maybe she thought she'd be able to change his mind.

Maybe he should have changed it, just so they could stay together.

Maybe he should have sold the farm and left North Dakota with her, and then his children would have a mom.

And he would have been miserable.

Would it have been better for his kids to grow up with a dad who worked a job he hated, but their family was still together?

If she left you when you were living in North Dakota, she'd leave you anywhere else.

That thought eased his guilt some. Because he figured that was probably right. She hadn't even really specifically mentioned the farming when she left. Just that she was sick of being married and taking care of children and babies and wanted to be free and single again. Wanted to be in the city where things were happening and she wasn't isolated.

She hadn't wanted the encumbrances of children and a husband and family.

"He looks happy."

Glory's voice startled him, and he looked away from Blanche and Daniel and Caleb, down into Glory's upturned face. He hadn't realized that the men had moved away and started cleaning the roasters. He had been that deep in thought.

Glory looked a little sad and maybe a little hurt as well.

"I was thinking about how she just walked away from her kids. Just wanted to be single. I don't understand how a responsible adult could do that. And then I guess I was also wondering why she's back."

"I wondered the same thing."

Maybe his words reassured her. He hated to think that she might have thought that he was staring at his ex, wishing they could get back together.

Just in case, he said, "I wish she'd leave. I...I was enjoying what was happening between you and me, and the relationship that you were developing with the kids. Her coming kind of messed it all up again. And, when she leaves, I'll be the one dealing with the kids who are crying about their mom, wondering where she went, why she doesn't want them."

"Do you think she's going to leave?" Rose asked, not sounding like she wanted her to or anything, just sounding like she wanted to know what he thought.

"I can't imagine she'd want to stay. Nothing has changed. There are still a bunch of little kids running around the house, still lots of laundry and dishes and cleaning and cooking to do. Still a lot of work from the time you get up in the morning until you go to bed at night. Nothing is different."

"Maybe she's changed."

He shifted, moving closer to Glory, wanting to put his arm around her, but not sure they were there yet. He glanced over at Blanche. "I haven't noticed anything that's changed."

"I guess I didn't know her that well before, to be able to say whether I have or not."

Feeling like he wanted to take a chance, or maybe he just wanted to touch her, he put his hand up, dropping it down on her shoulder and sliding it to her upper arm. He didn't exactly pull her to him, but he squeezed just a little.

She looked up, grinning at him. He supposed that meant she was okay with his touch.

"I had a good time today."

"I did too. I was kind of hoping maybe you'd go out with me some night this week. If Blanche is going to be here, we might as well take advantage of her babysitting."

Glory laughed out right at that. "I don't think Blanche is going to be very happy to hear that you're looking at her for babysitting. In fact, I think she might be downright upset about that."

"I guess I'm not really caring. They're her kids. It shouldn't even be called babysitting. A mother should be with her children because she wants to, not because anyone is asking or making her."

Maybe there was little heat in his words. Maybe he was a little angry about the fact that she didn't seem to care about the boys that he loved so much

"I thought you were going to try to get your barley planted this week. It's getting to the point where it needs to go in the ground or it's going to be too late."

"I know. The farm is important, it pays our bills, and supports our family, but I want to make time for you, too."

Her brows shifted down, and she looked slightly confused. Like the idea of putting the farm aside so that he could do something with her was a little bit confusing.

He doubted that was the reaction the Piece Makers were thinking he would get. He almost chuckled. It was exactly the reaction that *he* thought he would get. Maybe, if he and Glory went out, she would enjoy herself anyway. There was a part of him that wouldn't mind showing her a good time. Something off the farm.

Although for himself, he could have a good time at home any day of the week, a better time than if he went somewhere else.

But maybe that was part of the problem. Maybe he was just thinking about what he wanted, and what was best for him, and he wasn't thinking about the other person in the relationship.

He supposed, if he were being honest about it, he couldn't blame everything on Blanche. Because it was true. He hadn't wanted to leave the farm. Not that they talked about it. But that really wasn't something he wanted to compromise on, and, if he were going to find someone else, he would want to make sure they would be happy in North Dakota on a farm.

He could compromise on other things. Maybe he would rather stay home, but if the person he was with wanted to go out, he could do that.

Maybe he could try to be more thoughtful.

Not maybe. He could.

He could try to put himself in someone else's shoes, and think about how he would be feeling in their situation, and...like the Bible verse. *Do onto others as you would have them do unto you.*

How could he do onto others if he wasn't thinking about others? He needed to figure out what he would want in their situation, and then do it.

If he were Glory...she'd want to know for sure that if she were going to be in a relationship with him, he wasn't still pining over his ex.

That had been obvious to him.

She should expect special treatment from him. That he wasn't treating her the same as he treated others.

He could work on this. Maybe she'd even talk to him about it and help him. Give him a direction to go on, instead of him just trying to figure things out, like he was walking through the dark with no light.

"You seem like you're awfully thoughtful," Glory interrupted his thoughts once again.

"I guess I was just really looking forward to going out with you. Tomorrow we have field day at the school. Wednesday night is the auction. Tuesday?"

"Are you sure you'll get that barley planted?"

"I might be able to get it finished tomorrow. Or Tuesday before we go. Maybe we can plan on five?"

"Whatever time works for you."

"Let's do five. I'll make sure with Blanche that she'll be around. And if she's not, I know Ty and Louise's daughter would be happy to help. She was looking for babysitting jobs from what Ty was saying."

"I heard Louise talking about that as well. Like the girl doesn't have four little brothers to help with."

"They're not so little anymore. The youngest is in school with Benjamin."

"I guess you're right. I had them in Sunday School, and I still think of them as little kids. It's hard to believe they're growing up."

"Happens to the best of us."

Their eyes met, and he doubted she knew he was thinking that he wanted to be able to spend the rest of his life with her. That the older he got, the less time he'd have to spend with her.

Funny how he'd dated Blanche for a really long time and had trouble making up his mind as to whether or not she was the one he wanted to spend the rest of his life with. He'd asked her to marry him more because she seemed to expect it than because he really wanted to.

With Glory, he didn't have to think about it. He knew. She was the one. If she would have him.

Chapter 19

First, marry with lots of prayer and discernment, the very best man you can find; don't settle for anyone you are not 100% sure is God's will for your life. Second, realize he is a sinner just like you and love him through his rough moments and days even, and especially, when he doesn't deserve it. Hug and kiss every day. Be attentive to his desires and preferences and try to meet them. Laugh together often.
- Tabitha from New Britain, CT

Yesterday at the school's field day had been awkward.

Glory wasn't used to being the third part of a couple.

A couple who wasn't a couple. It felt odd to be there with Armstrong and his ex and their kids.

The kids had wanted their mom to watch everything, and while they had seemed to be getting used to her being around and had included Glory in their excitement more than they had at the hog roast, she still had felt like an outsider in their family.

Adam had included her, and had actually given his mother the cold shoulder, but Glory hadn't been any happier about that.

She didn't want the kids to not love their mother.

She just didn't want to be left out while they did. Which meant she would rather not be around.

Not that she was angry or upset, just that she felt like she was pushing into their family.

Regardless, the kids had done well, with Adam and Benjamin both winning ribbons. Adam's in the long run, and Benjamin's in the broad jump.

If they felt awkward with their oddly pieced together family, she couldn't tell. She supposed that was the important thing. Which is why she shoved her feelings aside after saying several times to Armstrong that she didn't need to be there, and he could spend the day with his family if he wanted to. He had insisted he wanted her, and that the kids did too.

Other than Adam, she wasn't sure about that, but she didn't argue, put her chin up, and decided she was going to have a good time.

Blanche had been hot and had wanted to sit in the shade a good bit, especially towards the end of the day, so sticking it out had worked in Glory's favor if she wanted to think about it like that. But she really didn't.

If she was going to be with Armstrong, his ex was a part of the package, and Glory was going to have to find a way to not feel unwanted, or like she was extraneous.

It was also natural for the children to want their mother. To love her.

It didn't seem to matter how terrible a person was as a parent, their children were just programed by God to love them.

Glory didn't want to change that at all. But it was just easier to do if she wasn't around to be passed over.

Still, it had been a good day, and Glory was glad she went.

Now she stood at the window watching Armstrong pull in in his pickup.

It was three o'clock in the afternoon, and the boys would be home from school soon. It was almost out for the year, and Glory had to admit she was looking forward to it.

She couldn't wait for them to be home all the time.

She always had a good time with the kids, and expected the summer to be a lot of fun.

"Is that the bus?" Blanche asked from the couch where she'd lain down for a nap after lunch. Her voice sounded sleepy and a little disinterested.

"No. It's Armstrong getting back with the pieces for his planter."

"Looks like you guys won't be going on a date after all. His barley isn't planted, and I know he's not going to want to stop and come in because it's supposed to rain tomorrow. You know how farmers are about the rain and getting work done before it gets muddy."

She seemed to be muttering under her breath, but Glory didn't really care. Some people just weren't cut out to work anything but nine to five.

And that was fine. That just wasn't her, and she knew it wasn't Armstrong, either. He had to plant when the time and weather cooperated.

She moved from the window, heading toward the refrigerator where she had a cucumber to cut up for the boys to snack on when they got home.

Blanche just stood in the doorway to the living room, staring at her.

"Can I get you something?" Glory asked, putting some cheer into her voice. She'd been cleaning the house this morning, and doing laundry and Blanche hadn't gotten up until almost noon so she hadn't really talked to her.

It seemed a little odd for someone to sleep so much, but she refrained from asking if she didn't feel well.

"I suppose if you want to get me a glass of water and a bowl of fruit I would eat it." Blanche walked to the table and sat down gracefully.

Glory bit her tongue. Why had she offered?

Because God calls you to be a servant.

Right, and God hated pride. It was her pride that wanted her to say 'go get your own stupid water. I'm not your maid.'

Those weren't words that would make the Lord happy. So, she got ice and put it in a glass, filled it up with water, and walked it over and set it on the table.

"Wow. You put ice in it," Blanche said, like she was expecting Glory to slam her drink down in front of her rudely.

Like she felt like doing.

Thankful that she hadn't gone with her feelings, she went back to get the fruit salad she had brought home from the hog roast on Sunday.

Nell from the other side of town had made it, and everyone had raved about it. Nell had a big family, and there was just a little left, not enough for her family, so she had given it to Glory. Everyone acted like Glory had won the lottery. Glory felt that way, because it had been really good. But she scraped the last of it out of the container filling a bowl and set it on the table in front of Blanche.

"Can I get you anything else?" she said calmly and as kindly as she could. After all, being a servant for one time wasn't what God had called her to.

He had called her to do it all of her life. To make it a lifestyle. Not to be nice when she felt like it, or when it suited her, or when she wasn't being made to feel like she was as low as dirt.

Blanche looked at her with narrowed eyes. "Why are you being so nice to me?" she asked, and she didn't sound very nice about it.

That made Glory's brows go up. She hadn't expected to be confronted after she had set the food and drink on the table for her.

"I guess it's because that's what God wants me to do." Her words were a little low and slow, and she felt guilty saying them, because she had *done* right, but she hadn't *been* right in her heart.

That was where God really wanted her to be right. In her heart, because that's what He saw. He judged her heart.

"Don't you have any kind of backbone? Your only desire is to be the little slave girl around here? Aren't you even going to make him marry you or are you just giving everything away for free?"

She waved her arm around, probably indicating the dishes and the cleaning and the clothes that Glory had been doing earlier.

Tempted to tell Blanche that she was being paid for her work, she closed her mouth. Even if Armstrong didn't pay her, she would be here because she owed him.

Plus, Armstrong wasn't paying her to wait on his ex. He would have told her to make his ex get her own drink. But...even though there probably wasn't a single person in the world who would have told her that she needed to wait on Blanche, she thought maybe God would have said something different.

He usually did.

Usually whatever the world was telling her to do wasn't the right thing.

"Are you feeling okay?" she asked gently. Hoping that she didn't sound like she was prying.

She definitely didn't want to pry, but she had noticed the dark circles under Blanche's eyes and thought back to how she had been sitting in the shade most of the day yesterday, and even at the hog roast, she'd been sitting down a good bit.

Glory had wanted to attribute that to laziness, but...maybe it was something else.

She took a tentative step toward the table unsure Blanche would confide in her even if there was something wrong.

"Why? Do I look sick?" Blanche asked, and she tried for a laugh, but it couldn't disguise the fear in her eyes.

"You seem tired. And I just thought maybe it was more than needing a little extra rest. Is it something I can help you with?"

"Unless you have a cure for stage IV pancreatic cancer, no."

Glory's eyes widened, and she couldn't keep the shock off her face.

"It's not like cancer isn't rampant in the world. And I just happen to be someone who was struck with dumb luck to get it."

"Aren't you getting treatments for it?"

"I could have. But they wouldn't work. The doctors told me they might extend my life by a few months, but I'd be miserable the whole time. It's hard to imagine being more miserable than I am right now, but I decided I wanted to go out with some class."

"Can I help you with that?" Glory heard herself asking. She hadn't wanted to. And, maybe in the back of her mind she was wondering if this would change Armstrong's mind.

Surely he would want to spend the last few months that Blanche had left with her. Maybe it would even soften his heart toward her and he'd remember all their good times together, and maybe they'd renew their vows and be a family until she passed.

Her imagination conjured up all sorts of scenarios where the man she seemed to be falling in love with ended up with someone else. Or at least ended up with someone else for a few months.

"Did they tell you how long you have left?" she asked, not just because she wanted to know how long Armstrong might be with his ex, but also because while Blanche looked tired, and maybe a little skinny now that she was really staring at her, she didn't seem like someone about to die.

"They gave me six months to a year, but I've heard that before with various other people, and usually when they say that, you've got a month. Two, tops."

"I see. So you wanted to come see your boys?"

Blanche looked down at the table, messing with the spoon that sat beside her uneaten fruit.

Finally she looked back up. "I lost my health insurance when I lost my job. It was too expensive for me to make the payments on it, and I was hoping I could stay here with hospice. I was hoping that...that Armstrong would pay for it."

Glory wasn't sure whether Armstrong would be able to afford that or not. But she knew she could donate her wages.

She didn't need to tell Blanche that, though.

Sweet Water would have fundraisers as well.

"I don't think you have anything to worry about. I'm pretty sure we'll take care of you here." She said that with confidence, knowing the town of Sweet Water, and the people in it.

Even if Blanche wasn't exactly a native son, and even if she left her husband and went off somewhere, they would do it because of Armstrong and his children. Because that's the kind of town they were.

"I wouldn't be so sure of it. I set up a 'go pay me,' and no one was interested. Everyone has their own things they want to spend money on, and they're not interested in paying for someone's hospice."

"You may be surprised."

Just then, Adam and Benjamin came in the door, and Glory realize she hadn't even heard the bus.

The boys munched on cucumbers while they told them about their day, and then she sent them upstairs to change their clothes quietly before they came back down.

"That's sneaky. You put sour cream out for them to dip their cucumbers in, and then they eat them."

"No. Actually, it was an accident that I found out that they like them. I was eating one myself one evening, and Caleb asked me for a piece. I just told him I didn't think he'd like it and he wouldn't want any. That seem to make the rest of them curious. They all kinda came over and stood and watched me. I didn't want them to waste any of my cucumber, so I wouldn't give them any. Finally, when they wouldn't leave, I cut one slice up into four little quarters, dipped it in some sour cream and handed it to them. They all loved it and asked for more. I ended up only getting the four pieces of the cucumber that I'd eaten before I shared it with the boys. They fell in love. That's our typical afterschool snack now."

"Wow. That's kind of amazing."

"That's what I thought. I'd never heard of kids who actually like cucumbers."

Blanche almost smiled, and Glory grinned at her, feeling like maybe they could be friends after all.

Not really because of Blanche's cancer, although maybe that did have something to do with it.

When a person had their health taken away from them, they realized that they really weren't as much in control of themselves and their lives as what they thought they were. It had a tendency to humble people. Glory had experienced that with a couple of her relatives who had been diagnosed with cancer.

It didn't really matter who you were, or what you had accomplished. You couldn't argue with the disease that ate you up from the inside.

Although, it was always a comfort to Glory to know that even cancer was no match for her God. And, if she were ever to get cancer, it would only be because God allowed it, according to His plan.

Of course, she thought it was probably wise to be as healthy as she could, because while God could control whether or not she was sick, as her health was in his hands, she could do her part.

And she would.

"If you don't mind, I'm going to walk outside and see if Armstrong will let me ride with him for a while on the tractor. I'll talk to him a bit, and I'm sure he'll be fine if you want to stay. We'll get the room I'm sleeping in ready, and you can have it."

"You'd move out of your room to sleep on the couch for me?"

"I sure would. Although, maybe you'll want to sleep downstairs on the couch. That way you won't have to climb the steps."

"I'm not that pathetically sick yet," Blanche said, rolling her eyes a little.

"No, of course not. When the time comes. If it comes. Maybe you'll have a miraculous recovery."

"Don't talk fairytales to me. I'm not going to recover. I just...don't want to be in a hospital. Have diapers. Lose my hair and look sick. I want to keep my dignity. If I'm going to have this disease, it's going to come to me on my terms."

Glory nodded. She could understand that, although she wasn't much of a fighter. Not like Blanche obviously was.

"I'll be here. I'm not so sick I can't watch my children."

Glory grinned. The corners of Blanche's mouth turned up and Glory felt like maybe they would end up friends.

Chapter 20

Communication, extending grace to each other.
- Paula Hurdle from Oxford, MS

Armstrong checked his watch, then looked at the field. He hadn't even gotten a quarter of it done. He hadn't expected his planter to break down yesterday evening, and of course the part that he needed wasn't in stock.

Thankfully, they had been able to order it in for today, but it still had taken most of the day before it was in, then he had to put it on before he could start planting again.

If he'd been able to work all day, he might have gotten most of the field finished.

As it was, he needed to stop in the next ten minutes so that he could go in and get ready to go. It was supposed to rain tomorrow.

There was a chance of rain on Thursday as well, and he might not get this barley in until next week.

He was already late.

Turning the planter at the end of the field, he watched the guide, lining the planter up and heading back down the field.

Glory walked toward him, cowgirl boots on, worn jeans, a blue T-shirt and the wind ruffling her hair and blowing it off to the side.

His heart skipped a couple of beats, and he figured that row was going to be crooked when he looked back down and saw that he'd turned the steering wheel inadvertently while he was staring at the woman he seemed to be falling in love with.

How could he not? After the way she treated him and his family, his boys, and even his ex.

She'd been gracious and sweet all day yesterday. It could have been a very awkward day, and maybe it was for her, because he caught a look on her face a couple of times like she wished she were somewhere else, but she seemed to have a good time, and her focus had been on making sure everyone else was enjoying themselves, and not on whether or not everyone was treating her right.

Which had convicted Armstrong, because he wasn't usually that considerate.

Maybe that's what the Piece Makers were talking about.

Idling the tractor down, he pushed the clutch in and took it out of gear, holding a foot on the break while he waited for Glory to finish walking up to him.

Maybe someday he'd get one of those big fancy tractors where he'd need to open the door in order for her to get in, but for now, he sat in the open sunshine, and was pretty happy that at least his tractor was paid for.

"Mind if I ride with you for a while?" she said as she stood beside the big back wheel, looking up at him and shadowing her eyes with her hand.

"I was just getting ready to stop. I need to have some time to take a shower and get ready to go."

"I thought we would have our date on the tractor today. Unless that'll disappoint you." She grinned at him.

"What if I was looking forward to a good steak?"

"You're taking me to a steakhouse? Okay never mind about that tractor ride," she said, acting like she was getting ready to turn around.

He laughed, and she looked back at him.

"It's supposed to rain tomorrow. Can we take a rain check on the date? Literally?"

It must have been the farming community who originated that statement, he figured as he nodded his head, words failing him.

That's what he needed. Someone who understood that it wasn't about his job coming first, necessarily. It was about getting things done when they needed to be done.

"You're promising me tomorrow?" he said, just to make sure.

"As long as it's raining," she replied cheerfully.

"Come on up. You just made this job look a whole lot nicer."

"I think he's calling me pretty," she said as she put one boot on the step and hopped up, settling on the fender well beside him.

"Sorry it's not real comfortable."

"I guess I'll just have to lean into you. Sorry about that."

"You know what, my ribs have hardly bothered me at all. I thought this might be a chore, but I took two Tylenol, and maybe that's what's doing it, but I'm feeling pretty good about it."

"That's great. I kind of feel like once they're through those first tender days, and they get some solid growth on them, it's not as important to baby them along."

"I was feeling the same thing. Although I definitely have my wrap on, too."

He started out again and tried to make sure he kept his row straight, even though Glory was a distraction.

"The kids were pretty tired when we got home yesterday, and there was a lot going on, and I never got to thank you for going with us. I appreciated it."

"It was my pleasure. I really had a great time. I mean, once I got over being awkward, and feeling a little bit weird, like I'm stepping in your family. But it turned out okay, and I'm really glad I went."

"I thought you might be struggling there for a bit. Thanks for pushing through it. I... I know that Blanche is the mother of my children, but she's not the one I want."

"I know. You said that, and I appreciate you saying it again. Sometimes I need reminded, because my doubts get in the way pretty easily, for some reason. About that especially. I struggled for a bit."

"I'll say it as often as you need me to. Because it's important to me that you know it."

"I don't think you need to be saying it too much." She cleared her throat and placed a hand on his shoulder, almost as though she needed a connection with him while she told him this next.

"Blanche just told me that she is dying of cancer. She thinks it's only going to be a month or two, although the doctors gave her six to twelve."

"You're kidding." He couldn't help it. He took his eyes off the rows and looked at her.

She was nodding and looked dead serious.

"Would Blanche lie about that?" he asked, thinking that Blanche hadn't looked like someone who was dying of anything.

"I don't think so. I actually noticed that she was sitting down more than maybe a normal person would. And the mean side of me wanted to think that she was being lazy, but, I finally asked her today if she was feeling okay. That opened up this conversation."

His mind was reeling. He didn't love her, and sometimes his feelings were more like hate, but he would never wish cancer or death on her. And she was the mother of his children.

Trying to get his thoughts in order, he said, "I suppose that's why she's back? She wanted to say goodbye to the kids?"

"That, and she needs us to take care of her. She doesn't have anyone else."

"What about her friends in the city?"

Glory shrugged and she didn't need to say if she had friends in the city that would help her, they'd be helping her, and she wouldn't be there with them.

He didn't say anything for a while. Figuring this was probably going to mess up what he wanted to do with Glory.

Then he figured that was selfish thinking, and he shouldn't be concerned about that. About himself and what he wanted.

"I guess I'll tell her that she can stay. We'll do the best we can with her. I... I don't expect you to become a caregiver. I'll have to figure that out."

"She lost her insurance. I think she was hoping that you might pay for hospice, but I figured that the town would pitch in. Also, instead of paying me, you could put my money towards a caregiver. I will help take care of her as well."

"I didn't bring you here to make you a slave in my home."

"I don't recall saying anything about feeling like a slave. I'm volunteering to do this, because I want to."

"You really don't owe me anymore."

"And I don't feel like I do. I like you. Can't I do some nice things for you and your family?"

Her words sounded a little hesitant, and he glanced over at her.

"I like you too. I suppose that's why I wanted to date you."

"That's a relief. I thought you were after my money."

"Oh? You have money? Well never mind about liking you then. Let's just get married."

"I think the Piece Makers would tell you that's not very romantic"

"I'm sure they would. I think the Piece Makers are going to give up on me. Not sure I can ever be what they want me to be."

"I think they just wanted us to get together. I think also, maybe the things they suggested you do weren't necessarily things that someone like me would like."

"Those are the only things I'm interested in. Things someone like you would like." He spoke immediately wanting her to know his intentions.

His words made her smile, and her hand moved a bit on his shoulder, almost in a caress.

They chatted the rest of the afternoon, and to his surprise he was able to finish the field even though he did the last three rows in the dark.

"Those last rows might be a little wobbly when the barley comes up, but at least it's in the ground."

"And ready for the rain tomorrow. That's about the best thing we could have done."

"You know, I really appreciate that. I... I don't want you to feel like you're not the most important thing, but I appreciate you understanding that I can't control the weather."

"And you can't control whenever your ribs are going to be broken by a cow either. We just have to go with it sometimes."

He closed the barn door behind him, but instead of walking toward the house, he took her hand.

"Are you sure you're okay if Blanche stays with us?"

"I am. I wouldn't want to do it any other way. I think your boys will appreciate being able to spend her last days with her. It might not be pretty, but they'll remember that they had this time."

He nodded. "I agree."

Some people might think they'd need to be herded away, so they don't see anything that might upset them, but he wasn't one of the people who believe that. Kids needed to see life, and sometimes life wasn't pretty. Sometimes it involves death.

In their culture, they tended to shield themselves from death, like by shielding themselves it didn't happen, or wasn't there.

He was of the mind that it was better to be prepared for it. Spiritually.

And part of that was living the kind of life where when he was looking at the end of it, he didn't look back with regrets and sorrow.

"Thanks for riding with me. I think that's the most fun I've ever had on a tractor." Maybe that was a corny line, but it was still the truth.

"Me too," she said, grinning up at him, and he could never see her smiling without wanting to smile back.

They stared at each other, him holding onto her hand, before his hand came up, touching her cheek. Maybe he should have said something. Had some kind of pretty words to tell her, but he didn't.

He just lowered his head toward hers and kissed her softly. It felt sweet and right and he didn't want it to be short, but he didn't want to push her either, and he was going to pull back, but she moved forward, lifting her head up, and putting her arms around his neck, running her fingers into his hair and pulling his head down further, deepening the kiss, and he found that all thoughts of a short kiss fled.

In fact, he kind of wanted it to last forever.

It didn't, of course, but it was still the best kiss of his life, and, while he didn't want it to end, it left him with a smile that he couldn't contain as they walked to the house together, hand in hand.

Life probably wasn't going to be easy, especially the next few months, but it certainly looked a lot brighter since he knew Glory would be beside him through it all.

Epilogue

"I now pronounce you man and wife," Pastor Cummings said as he stood in front of Glory and Armstrong in their living room, Blanche on the couch and their children standing behind them.

Armstrong smiled at his bride and lowered his head as she lifted her.

Calhoun had pretty much given up getting to the alter himself, but it was nice to see Armstrong and Glory so happy.

Armstrong and he had become pretty good friends over the past month as Calhoun had come and done some repairs to the house, then had made the light-therapy box Glory had requested for Blanche.

Funny that Glory and Blanche got along so well. For all that Blanche was Armstrong's ex, and from what Calhoun had heard, she hadn't been overly kind to Glory when she'd first come back. But Glory had gone out of her way to love her, to the point of taking care of her as she slowly faded away from cancer.

Actually, Glory had researched alternative treatments and had Blanche on a special diet and taking a ton of supplements. Calhune wasn't sure it was going to work to save her life, but Blanche had gone from being unking to Glory to singing her praises every chance she got. They were lifelong friends, for sure, although Calhune wasn't sure how long Blanche's life was going to be.

The entire downstairs of the house was crowded with friends and neighbors, making it warmer than was strictly comfortable, and Calhune pulled at the collar of his button up.

"I heard you're a pretty good carpenter," a voice behind him said, making him turn.

"I don't know about that, but most of the time the stuff I build stays together, anyway," Calhune said as Remington Martinez held out a hand, which he shook.

"That's about all anyone can ask for," Rem said, his arm around his small, blond-haired wife.

Calhune nodded, thinking he'd ask how the renovations were coming with Rem and Elaine's vacation rentals. Calhune had heard that the movie star who was coming after Thanksgiving had been insisting on a lot of changes.

Before he could ask about them, Rem said, "I'm looking for a carpenter. If you can do wiring and plumbing work, I'd pay you double."

"I can. But if you're talking about your rentals, I've heard the movie star is difficult to work with."

"You heard right. But the amount we're getting paid is making it worth it to cater to her. Thing is, I'm having trouble keeping workers. Nolt told me you can pretty much get along with anyone. Right now, that's what we need."

Calhune didn't say anything for a couple of minutes. This time of year, his family was always busy, and come harvest time, it would be even more so. But he'd never been back to Rem and Elaine's rentals, although he'd heard the area was gorgeous, rugged and secluded. He wouldn't mind spending some time in such a place, and even having a hand in fixing it up.

"What are you thinking?" he finally asked.

Rem launched into the repairs that the starlet had demanded, the little luxuries and the things she'd complained about when she'd sent her agent out to take pictures for her.

All things that were well within Calhune's skill set.

"Let me talk to my brothers and dad and see if they can live without me for a while. I might need to do some now and finish up after harvest season."

"I understand. I suppose the biggest requirement is the ability to not get offended if what you do doesn't suit the queen-elect."

"Rem," Elaine chided softly.

"Sorry. I forgot Her Highness is only a royal princess." Rem's amused gaze met his wife's reproachful look. The easy laughter between them and the clear love they shared made Calhune restless. Like if he just looked hard enough, he'd find something like that, too.

Take the job.

The words were clear in his head. So clear, he almost looked around to see who said them. But the murmurs and laughter of the wedding guests hadn't abated, and no one was talking to him.

God? I can't leave my family without help.

He couldn't just up and take another job without checking with them first.

Take the job.

Same clear tones, even though they weren't audible.

He supposed he'd just made the Lord tell him twice. He wouldn't make him say it a third time.

"As long as it's okay with my family, I'll do it."

"You don't want to come see what all it entails?" Elaine asked, her brows raised high.

"No. I'm sure this is a job I need to take, but I'm not sure why." He wasn't going to try to explain the audible voice. Rem and Elaine were understanding people, but maybe not quite that understanding.

"Don't talk him out of it, Elaine. There aren't any other men in all of North Dakota who can do wiring, plumbing and carpentry, and actually also have a chance of getting along with Bellamy Levine."

Calhune barely saw the loving glance the couple shared. Bellamy Levine. Known as a modern-day Elizabeth Taylor, she'd been married five times and her latest break-up had made national news headlines for weeks as she and her action hero husband fought over everything from the drapes to the dog to the ice cream in the freezer.

Calhune didn't even know any movie stars, since he barely ever watched any movies, but even he had heard of Bellamy. No last name necessary.

Maybe Rem saw the doubt on his face. "You already said you'd do it," he reminded Calhune.

Take the job.

Third time, Lord. I get it.

"I'm not backing out. If later today suits you, I'll be out so you can show me what needs done."

"It does." There was no hesitation in Rem's voice and Calhune smiled.

If she got married five times, she must be nice, at first, anyway.

"Alright, I'll see you later," Calhune said and Rem and Elaine were pulled away by their children who wanted to talk to them about something.

Okay, Lord. I'm not sure what Your plan is, but I know it involves me doing work at Rem and Elaine's vacation spot.

Maybe whatever the Lord had planned involved him learning some new skills he'd need when he built his own home on the property he'd just bought not far outside of Sweet Water. It had no improvements on it at all, so he had his work cut out for himself. But he hadn't been in any hurry. After all, there was still hope he'd find a woman to share it with him.

Not a movie star. And definitely not one who had been married five times. He wanted a woman who was comfortable on a farm and just fun to be around. Not someone who had plenty of practice getting divorced and plenty of money to pay divorce lawyers.

Send me a nice girl, Lord. Please.

Enjoy this preview of *Cowboy Stealing My Heart,* just for you!

Cowboy Stealing My Heart

Chapter 1

Communication, extending grace to each other.
- Paula Hurdle from Oxford, MS

T he sports car missed his toe by an inch.

Calhoun Powers jerked his head up from his phone. He should have been paying attention. But he'd been eager to let his brother know that he'd found the O-ring they needed at Sweet Water's hardware store and they wouldn't need to order it in to finish the rebuild they were doing on a turbo.

But it was Sweet Water. There was never any traffic. The traffic that they did have took it nice and slow through town.

Not this sports car.

Out-of-state plates.

California.

That explained everything.

Calhoun's lips pursed as brake lights came on, tires squealed, and the car stopped before the reverse lights came on, and it backed up.

He stood in front of his pickup, waiting for the driver to do whatever they were going to do before he hopped in and headed back to the garage.

The car stopped in front of him.

Dude probably wanted directions.

The tinted window slowly went down, and from the angle he was looking at, he saw a long, slender leg.

It wasn't a dude.

He took a step back and lowered his head slightly, looking in the window to meet the eyes of the driver.

Wasted effort, since she wore huge, dark sunglasses, that took up most of her face.

Long golden blonde hair poured down her back and over both shoulders.

There was something familiar...

Calhoun's eyes lifted slightly from the woman, looking over her low-slung car at the movie theater that was directly across the street.

Usually they played movies that were several months old or even older.

But the entire town had been abuzz, along with the rest of the country, about the brand-new romantic comedy that was set to release in the next week.

The highest-paid actress in Hollywood was in it, and her leading man was the man that she just had a one-million-dollar divorce settlement with.

Their chemistry on-screen was supposed to be sizzling, even though they'd been fighting and barely speaking to one another off-screen.

It was such a big deal that the owners of Sweet Water's movie theater had actually bitten the bullet, paid the high fees, and ordered the movie in.

Figuring that even a small theater like them would be able to make their money back on such a huge movie.

The poster for that movie took up the entire front window.

The actress on the poster was smiling coyly and had her finger wrapped around the tie of the actor standing across from her.

The lady in the car wasn't smiling and didn't look coy, but there was something familiar about her, and Calhoun searched the poster for just another second before his eyes dropped back down to the woman in the car.

"Can I help you, ma'am?" he drawled, putting a little more country in his words than was strictly necessary. He wasn't sure why, other than he didn't want her to mistake him for anything other than what he was, which was a blue-collar dude who might be able to work on her car but would never drive one as fancy as that.

He could build her house, but he'd never live in it.

That thought came to him, since he had been renovating the vacation rentals for Rem and Elaine Martinez, one of them just for some big Hollywood hotshot.

Maybe that was this lady.

She didn't bother to lower her glasses, but she did manage to look down her nose at him when she said, "I'm looking for the Martinez vacation rentals. My GPS seems to have quit working."

"It does that around here," he said, and there was no sympathy in his voice. Hard to dredge up any feeling of compassion when she obviously had everything she could ever want at her fingertips.

He ought to know, since he'd spent the last month turning one of Rem's rustic cabins into the lap of luxury. For him, anyway, since it included a jetted hot tub, a massive large-screen TV, skylights, stainless steel appliances, wall-to-wall tile in the bathroom and kitchen, as well as voice-activated lighting and heating.

Each request had seemed more ridiculous than the last, as they came in one by one. Almost as though the woman were changing her mind, needing more and more in order for her to retreat to the country.

"Well?" the woman in front of him said, irritation in her tone.

"Well, what?" he asked, wondering if she thought that he was going to somehow be able to fix her GPS. He wasn't a magician.

"Can you give me directions to Martinez vacation rentals, or should I ask someone a little higher on the evolutionary ladder?"

He grunted, not because he needed to make a noise, but because he clamped his teeth over the "yes" that wanted to come out. Just because this woman rubbed him the wrong way didn't mean he needed to be rude.

He forced a pleasant, if small, smile on his face. "Keep going straight out of town. Just follow this road for about thirty miles. There'll be a right-hand turn and a little wooden sign with white lettering and an arrow. The name of the road is Convenient Marriage, and you'll just follow that back until you see the rentals." He nodded his head in that direction and then figured he'd better add, "If you need to talk to Rem, you have to stop at the house which isn't far off Convenient Marriage Lane on the left."

The woman pursed her lips and somehow looked like she was smiling and holding her nose at the same time. "Thank you. Do I need to pay you?"

He almost thought she was asking that question as an insult, but he supposed he wasn't sophisticated enough to be offended.

He just shrugged and said, "No."

He had no desire to continue a conversation with her and even less to try to figure out what was offensive about what she had just said.

She looked smug.

She didn't look away, although her finger moved slightly, and the dark tinted passenger window glass slowly closed.

Calhoun didn't wait for it to shut the whole way before he straightened and took a step back, ready to get in his truck and pull out as soon as her car was no longer in his way.

He didn't have to wait for long, as she took off quickly. The tires didn't squeal, but he figured it was just a miscalculation on her part.

Walking around the front of his pickup, he'd gotten a hand on the latch when his phone rang.

Pulling it out of his pocket, he climbed in before he answered. "Hello?"

"Calhoun. It's Rem. I have a favor to ask of you."

"Go ahead," Calhoun said easily. He'd been doing favors for Rem for over a month as the big movie star had been changing orders right and left. Calhoun didn't mind, because Rem was paying him well.

He had been planning on working on the cabins today, but his family had gotten their show truck in the garage, and he was the only one who could put hardwood floor down in the cab. Then he'd gotten roped into a couple of other projects, but he figured it didn't matter, since his dad knew the day after next he'd be moving up to Rem's to work full-time on the cabins over the holidays. Rem wanted them finished before the spring tourist season started, and things were usually slow at the garage over the holidays for his family anyway.

His brother Silas was the one who did all the motor repairs, although Calhoun had done his share of helping, since tearing down a motor and rebuilding it was a lot of work.

His brother Flynn kept the numbers for the company, but he also was the one who did all the painting. It took a steady hand and a ton of patience in order to do it right.

Any carpentry work, including redoing entire interiors, fell to Calhoun. He just had a knack for those kinds of things.

"I got a call from my family in Texas, and I need to go down early. We were planning on going down for Thanksgiving and staying through Christmas and New Year's, but my mom fell and broke her hip, and I'm going to take the family down so we can give a hand on the ranch and also help with her care."

"That's fine," Calhoun said. "I hope she heals up fast," he added, figuring he ought to at least say something along those lines.

"She's tough. I'm sure she'll be fine. But I just want to make sure that you'd be okay continuing with the work that you're doing, and I was also wondering if you might be interested in taking care of my guest. There's just one of her, and as far as I understand it, she wants to be left alone, so she shouldn't give you too much trouble. Of course, you can stay out there like you were planning on doing, living in the big cabin while you're working on the others."

"It definitely makes it easier. I can just get up and go to work. If I'm going to be at some movie star's beck and call, it might be nicer if I don't have to drive forty minutes to get there every time she needs something."

Rem laughed. "What makes you think she's going to be high maintenance?"

"Oh, I don't know. Maybe the fact that she's changed everything she wanted at least four times and has been rather demanding every time."

He didn't mention that he'd met her and figured it was her typical personality to expect the world to wait on her hand and foot.

Rem laughed again. "At least you're getting paid well."

"That's what I tell myself every time. Although, it is kind of frustrating to do a job, only to rip it up and have to do a different job. I think there are mental institutions for people who are forced to do that type of thing."

"Sometimes I think a mental institution would be a nice break from real life." Rem's voice held sage wisdom.

"I guess I haven't gotten to that point in my life, old man," Calhoun said, just rubbing it in that Rem was a good decade or so older than he was.

"The married life, not age," Rem said, then under his breath, he said, "Ouch!"

Elaine said something in the background, and Calhoun laughed. Rem and Elaine had the type of relationship that he would love to have. After more than a decade of marriage, they still smiled at each other and held hands and seemed to admire and respect each other.

It was fun to watch them interact, even though Calhoun wouldn't have called himself much of a romantic.

He wouldn't mind getting married. Settling down. Having someone to greet him when he came home at night. A companion, a friend, someone to walk through life with him.

"I don't mind taking care of things while you're gone. As long as I'm not going to be held responsible when your Hollywood starlet decides North Dakota is too much for her, and she runs back home to the city."

He knew Rem wouldn't hold it against him. Even if it was entirely his fault. Rem was a good man. He would never expect Calhoun to not offend someone who was bound and determined to be offended.

"Yeah. Her payment is nonrefundable twenty-four hours before she arrives, and that's today. So the money's in the bag. Not that I don't think we ought to do our best to give her what she wants. She's paid a lot of money, but after what you've been through the last month, twisting yourself into a pretzel in order to do all the things she demands, I know you're up for it."

Calhoun wasn't sure. It was one thing to do carpentry work for someone who was a thousand miles away.

It was another thing to be woken up in the middle of the night because she wanted him to get an extra blanket out of the trunk at the foot of the bed. Or something equally ridiculous.

Still, Rem had paid him well, and he was sure that would continue, so he supposed he could manage to put up with a little inconvenience.

"I don't want to take you from the trucking company if you're needed there, so don't feel obligated."

"It's good. Things have been pretty quiet, other than this last truck that just came in. It's doing the normal winter slowdown. We'll be hauling feed, but harvest is over and freight slows down until January."

That was the way it was every year, which made it nice in some ways but also made it almost seem like a seasonal job in others, where there was not enough work to keep everyone busy, but there was too much to lay anyone off.

He supposed winter was meant to be a resting time.

"Sounds good. I won't be back until after the new year, but if you can't do it that long, just let me know. Make yourself at home, treat it like it's yours." Rem's words were casual, with the confidence that came from a man who knew he was talking to someone he could depend on.

"Thanks. If I run into any issues, I know your number."

"And you also know how to handle them. I'm not worried about a thing. I trust you."

They hung up a couple minutes later, and Calhoun started his pickup.

It wasn't quite ten in the morning yet. He'd finished the floor and just had a small repair job to do. He could make it out to the resort area tonight, most likely.

He really loved it out where the resort was. There was a beautiful lake, pine trees, rolling hills. Pretty views, and nice and secluded. He'd rigged up some solar panels that provided limited electricity, enough for lights and small appliances. The major appliances—washer, dryer, water heater—were gas.

Some of the cabins which were scattered around the lake were rustic enough to not have any of that stuff, just enough room for a bed. They were perfect if someone wanted to rent one for a fishing trip or just to get away from it all.

But the starlet's cabin had been expanded and fully furnished. And refurnished.

Something told him that she might be a pain in the butt.

But another voice said that there was probably a reason she was trying to get away; her divorce—and all the bad press that had been going along with that—would be one of those things. So maybe she'd just want to be by herself.

He could only hope.

Pick up your copy of Cowboy Stealing My Heart by Jessie Gussman today!

A Gift from Jessie

View this code through your smart phone camera to be taken to a page where you can download a FREE ebook when you sign up to get updates from Jessie Gussman! Find out why people say, "Jessie's is the only newsletter I open and read" and "You make my day brighter. Love, love, love reading your newsletters. I don't know where you find time to write books. You are so busy living life. A true blessing." and "I know from now on that I can't be drinking my morning coffee while reading your newsletter – I laughed so hard I sprayed it out all over the table!"

Made in the USA
Middletown, DE
03 March 2023

26101085R00106